Stroke of Death

Just then a blackbird appeared on the hedge. In its beak, held insecurely because of its size, there hung a large crust of bread. Lucy watched, amused by the bird's struggle to bear away such a prize from some neighbouring garden. The sparrows watched too, waiting for the prize to fall, not daring to act until this happened. Mr Lawrence watched, the trembling left hand moving very slowly upward and out towards the table.

The blackbird, hovering uncertainly over the hedge, could hold its heavy burden no longer. It tried to fly on, jerked twice up and down and dropped its prize on the centre of the table. Mr Lawrence's hand swept across and across. The birds flew off in a fright. The shaking hand closed on the bread, was drawn back and with eager, clumsy speed crammed the prize into the lop-sided mouth, already open to receive it.

Other titles in the Walker British Mystery Series

JOSEPHINE
BELL
Stroke
of
Death

WALKER AND COMPANY · NEW YORK

First published in the United States of America in 1977 by the
Walker Publishing Company, Inc.

This paperback edition first published in 1984.

ISBN: 0-8027-3073-6

Library of Congress Catalog Card Number: 77-79963

Printed in the United States of America

10   9   8   7   6   5   4   3   2   1

1

LUCY SUMMERS SLOWED her small car outside the tall hedge, then pulled in tight to the kerb, stopped the engine and got out.

She had seen the name in black letters on the gate half-way along the hedge. The Old Farmhouse. The gate, being low and narrow, was almost buried in the hedge that had grown wider as well as taller as it developed. Or perhaps, she thought, as she walked from the car, this was a new one set back from the footpath on purpose. For the hedge was undoubtedly old, not at all in keeping with the modern suburban gardens she had passed on her way to it. Well-laid-out, moneyed suburbia, she had thought, very open to the public gaze with its little pools and careful stone-work among the well-stocked beds and trim grass. The Old Farmhouse preserved a former tradition with success. Until she passed in through the little white gate Lucy could not see the house at all, only grass and very dignified, elderly trees.

The path took her round a sharp bend to the right, and there was the house; nothing spectacular, not very large, though bigger than its young neighbours; two-storied, solid, in a pleasantly mature brick. Of no definite period, it yet conveyed a respectable age, a continuous mild development. It suited its name.

Lucy found a bell push in the white-washed porch and pressed it hopefully. There was no answer. She tried again.

She even lifted and dropped the heavy, rusted old knocker at the centre of the door. This made a formidable noise for which she felt instant shame and some alarm. But still nothing happened.

All right, she thought, so they're out in spite of being warned to expect me. So I've wasted time and petrol coming out here, but I don't pay for them. Poor old tax-payer. Lousy old patient asking for treatment and not being at home when it arrived.

She pulled out her notebook, took a folded list from it and discovered which client she was due to see after this one. Then with a final unproductive attempt upon the door, she turned to go.

Moving, as she had, along the path from the gate, she had not seen any of the garden except that part of it leading to the house. But now the area that had been behind her and to her left as she approached the front door was now in clear view. Still no flower-beds of the suburban type, no riot of colour, but some flowering shrubs, lilac and viburnum in flower, laburnum and rhododendron with buds just breaking. In the sunny corner at the hedge boundary there was a rose-festooned arch with, near it, a bird-table on one side and on the other a wheelchair, occupied.

Her patient, old Mr Lawrence, she realised, parked comfortably in the sunny, charming, old-world garden, where he could watch and hear the birds, even if he could not whistle to them.

For her notes told her that Mr Lawrence had suffered a brain haemorrhage two months ago and was paralysed on the right side, with loss of speech. He was over seventy and had made little progress since the stroke; not able to walk, no recovery of his speech. He was living with his son and daughter-in-law at The Old Farmhouse, a family property. The three of them had come there only quite recently. Their doctor in Meadowfield belonged to a group practice. As a trained physiotherapist of the ambulatory type, not working in a hospital, Lucy had been attached

6

to this group. Dr Harris, the youngest partner in it, had asked her to investigate Mr Lawrence's present state and progress.

"Poor old boy can't explain his symptoms," Dr Harris had told her. "Ought to have got a bit mobile by now, according to his last notes from the registrar at Lincoln where he had his stroke. Very frustrated, of course. See what you think of him. His daughter-in-law is very co-operative, but anxious, Nurse Partridge tells me."

So here Lucy was, in the garden of the patient's house, with no means of introducing herself to him except the crude, perhaps startling one of appearing suddenly at his side. Well, not suddenly, because he might not have the power of speech, but presumably he could both hear and see. So if she made a reasonably noisy advance, even called out to him when she came into view, to explain who she was, might it not be a good opportunity to get to know him a little or would he be upset and then the young Mrs Lawrence would be angry, perhaps complain, perhaps even —

Lucy was young, twenty-two, fresh from her carefully-guided training and hospital experience. But she was keen, with a quick observant mind and a character as robust as her physique. Experience and the normal routine monotony of any profession or craft still had not blunted her lively curiosity. She made up her mind, left the porch and advanced carefully in the direction of the wheelchair.

But before she reached the halfway point on the lawn she stopped, fascinated, slightly disturbed, by what she saw.

Old Mr Lawrence had his eyes fixed on the bird-table which, she now realised, was within arm's length of his wheeled chair. Well within, she saw, for he was reaching over its rough wooden top. Evidently the birds were well used to him, for though they fluttered and hopped away from the moving fingers, they did not fly off and when the

7

hand withdrew they were back at once pecking busily at the invisible, tiny fragments of fat and breadcrumbs.

Poor old man, Lucy thought, trying to stroke them, was he? Trying to make contact with small friends who did not need speech to communicate, who clearly understood his feeble advances, were not hostile, held no menace.

She continued to stand and watch, unwilling to interrupt an activity the old man clearly found absorbing. Just then a blackbird appeared on the hedge. In its beak, held insecurely because of its size, there hung a large crust of bread. Lucy watched, amused by the bird's struggle to bear away such a prize from some neighbouring garden. The sparrows watched too, waiting for the prize to fall, not daring to act until this happened. Mr Lawrence watched, the trembling left hand moving very slowly upward and out towards the table.

The blackbird, hovering uncertainly over the hedge, could hold its heavy burden no longer. It tried to fly on, jerked twice up and down and dropped its prize on the centre of the table. Mr Lawrence's hand swept across and across. The birds flew off in a fright. The shaking hand closed on the bread, was drawn back and with eager, clumsy speed crammed the prize into the lop-sided mouth, already open to receive it.

Lucy was astonished, horrified, confused. Mr Lawrence had pounced as eagerly, and because of his superior size and human cunning, more successfully than the sparrows would have done if his action had not driven them away. He had behaved like any other creature, animal, bird, child, that saw food, wanted to grab it, stuff it in, munch it, swallow it. Mr Lawrence was still munching: from behind, even ten paces behind him where Lucy still stood frozen, she could see the ancient jaw-line moving, the old scalp with its sparse white thatch, twitching.

She wanted to go away. It would be easy to do so without at all disturbing this strange, very abnormal, rather disgusting patient. No one could blame her for going. Young Mrs Lawrence had not kept the appointment. So many of them had no sense of time. The old boy had not heard her advance. Naturally, he was too intent on his queer game — if it was a game, or just part of his infirmity.

But it had been more than a game. It had been no less than a sudden dread revelation of universal naked want, the basic need of the living universe. Lucy, unwilling, shrinking from truth, yet felt compelled to accept it. Angrily, she pushed out of her mind all those grandiose, pompous words she had read and been taught about the living universe and its needs. She had seen something stark and simple. No game. A fact. Hunger. Mr Lawrence was *hungry*. Why?

"Good morning, Mr Lawrence," Lucy said, moving round the wheelchair to face the old man. "I am a physiotherapist. I have been asked to see if I can help to improve your walking."

She was wearing navy-blue slacks, a jacket to match, a white jumper. No badge. No exact uniform. But she took it for granted he would understand what she meant. He must have had plenty of physiotherapy in hospital judging by those notes from Lincoln. She saw that he did indeed recognise her profession and also that he welcomed her arrival.

"I'm afraid your daughter-in-law isn't in. I did ring the bell and knock. I expect you heard me?"

He nodded and waved his left hand outwards and back. "You thought I'd given up and gone away, I suppose?"

Again he nodded and tried to smile. His faded old eyes beamed at her, which made the twisted shape of the smile more pitiful, because genuine, not just a remembered courtesy. Anyway, he must have been a real good-looker when he was young, she thought. And tall, perhaps athletic, certainly no soft fat about him, too thin, if anything. She

9

remembered the crust on the bird-table. The general run of her patients — her clients, the Social Service women liked to call them — were usually over- rather than under-nourished. Was Mr Lawrence's spare appearance part of his illness or was he, for some reason, lacking the necessary intake of food?

All this ran through the back of her mind as she asked him a few routine questions and wrote down the answers in the form of nods or shakes of the head. It was a late May day, with only a few thin clouds high up, streaking the bright blue of the sky. The sun shone warmly into the corner of the garden. Mr Lawrence, Lucy noticed, had pushed away the rug that covered his knees.

"Would you like to show me how much you can do in the way of walking?" the girl asked. "The lawn here is nice and flat. Without your sticks or your aid — You must tell — I mean show — "

She stopped, cursing her tactless babble, flushing red, catching her lower lip in her teeth. But Mr Lawrence only shook his head sadly, seeming to forgive her as well as to explain that he had neither sticks nor walking aid of any kind.

"So shall we try a few steps?" Lucy asked and getting no response at all added, "Or even just practise standing up and sitting down?"

The old man lifted his left shoulder in what was meant to be a shrug, then nodded his head slowly several times.

"Good," said Lucy. "I promise I won't let you fall. We'll try standing up first and then see how we go from there."

Feeling already too warm, far too warm, partly from her recent embarrassment, but chiefly from the sun in that sheltered corner, Lucy pulled off her jacket, which she had already unbuttoned while she was talking. Not fancying the bird-table as a suitable resting place for the garment, she dropped it in a heap on the grass beside the wheelchair. As it fell two wrapped bars of chocolate

10

rolled out of a pocket, landing almost under the foot-rest. As Lucy stooped to recover them, Mr Lawrence pounced.

The girl did not see him move, so quick was he, until their heads met in a smart collision. While Lucy started back with a cry of pain, the old man scooped together the chocolate bars in his shaky left hand and transferred them to a pocket before using the hand to clutch the side of the chair and haul himself back into a sitting position.

The struggle was brief, a few seconds only. Lucy, dazed, indignant, one hand on the bird-table to steady herself, watched Mr Lawrence plunge his hand into his side pocket, drag out a chocolate bar and push it, gaudy wrapping and all, into his mouth.

"You can't!" Lucy panted. "You mustn't! Not the paper as well!"

Mr Lawrence, eyes flashing, grinned at her. Liquid chocolate was running down his chin, together with bits of wrapping paper that he had begun to spit out.

"You very naughty old so-and- — old *gentleman*!" Lucy cried, but he continued to munch and spit and in a few seconds the useful left hand was moving jerkily towards the pocket and the second choc-bar.

"Let me unwrap it for you," Lucy begged. She would have to clean up the mess he had made of his shirt front with the first bar. Her own fault for having them in her pocket at all, instead of putting them with the rest of her lunch which was in the car. No good letting him make a worse mess with the second one.

He looked at her, all suspicion, unwilling to hand over his prize, but feeling grateful for the inner comfort that had begun to spread through his being.

"It was part of my lunch, you know," Lucy told him, still holding out her hand. "Not that I want it back now. I usually have lunch in the car, by the roadside. In the country, if possible, on my round. Come on! Hand over!"

Reluctantly, still suspicious, he did so and she took off the wrapping and gave the bar back to him. He crammed it, whole, into his mouth. This time there was no dribbling, no loss of the precious stuff. He ate it very carefully indeed, then leaned back, his eyes smiling his thanks, though his mouth trembled as he searched the crannies of his few teeth for any remaining fragments of delicious chocolate.

"Just look at your shirt," Lucy scolded. "And your jacket, too. I can't leave you looking like this, can I?"

Glancing down at himself, Mr Lawrence's dismay was obvious. "I need some water," Lucy went on, "and I can't get into the house to fetch some, so I'll have to wait here until Mrs Lawrence gets back, won't I?"

He shook his head so violently that she thought he would break his neck. The stark fear in his eyes startled her more than any of the rest of his strange behaviour. She looked about her: no small suburban pond, no outside tap in view. But the old man was waving that shaky left hand again. The bird-bath, occupying the middle of the bird-table. A film of scum on it. Well, what the hell, the whole set-up was as crummy as they come, surely?

"It's not very nice water, is it?" she said, rather crossly. "But I suppose it'll have to do. Where's your handkerchief?"

He pointed to his jacket pocket, then shook his head violently again, waving his hand as before. Lucy sighed, searching her large handbag for that second handkerchief she always carried. With this she set to work.

Remembering her own early childhood she made him spit on the clean linen, then wiped the smears of chocolate off his face with it. Next, dipping the handkerchief into the bird-bath she attacked the stains on his shirt and jacket and soon had the brown marks rubbed away, leaving clear wet patches.

At that moment they both heard the garden gate open and bang shut. Lucy glanced up. The fear was back in Mr Lawrence's eyes, worse than ever: panic fear and added to it a piteous appeal that struck at Lucy's heart.

She understood. The brown-stained handkerchief! Stuffing it into a trouser pocket she moved quickly, so that she stood between the old man and the gate and the approaching footfalls. She plucked his handkerchief from the pocket he had indicated before, reached across to wet it and had just begun again to wipe his shirt when a pleasant, surprised voice said, "Well, you seem to be very busy, Miss — Summers, isn't it?"

Lucy shot upright with scarlet cheeks. She saw a slim-figured woman, very neatly dressed, in a heavy linen, lime-green trouser suit, with carefully waved, modestly dyed brown hair and fashionable, but not extreme make-up on a thin, deeply lined face. An intelligent face, Lucy thought, with quick, cold eyes that missed nothing, but did not actively repel.

"Yes, I am Lucy Summers. Physiotherapist. I called at the time I was given."

"My wretched hairdresser." The woman interrupted any further explaining. "I am Mrs Lawrence, as I'm sure you have guessed."

"Of course."

Lucy felt calmer. Also relieved to be meeting someone with whom she could communicate freely and normally. "You must forgive me for introducing myself to my patient. I saw him from the front door when I discovered you were out. So I walked over and explained who I was."

Mrs Lawrence nodded. She had not looked at Lucy during this explanation but at the old man in the chair. He in his turn had kept his gaze upon Lucy. The fear was still in his eyes and a tension with it now that she found terrifying.

"You must have startled him I'm afraid," said Mrs Lawrence softly. "His shirt — ?"

She turned her green-ringed eyes on Lucy.

"What in the world has he been doing, Miss Summers?"

Lucy handed her the wet handkerchief, which she took with reluctance and at once dropped upon the grass.

13

"I'm afraid he did get a little excited," Lucy said. "He began dribbling — they can't help it, as I'm sure you know. So I used his handkerchief to mop him up."

"With the water in the bird-bath, I see," said Mrs Lawrence, still in the same pleasant co-operative voice.

"Yes."

Lucy picked up her bag.

"I must be getting on, Mrs Lawrence. I'm so glad I was able to see you. May I visit Mr Lawrence indoors on Friday, when I come again? Will that be convenient? About the same time? Dr Harris thinks his treatment should be more positive. The standing and walking, I mean."

"He can do neither," said Mrs Lawrence sadly. She took the bar of the wheelchair and swung it round, not roughly, but without giving the old man any notice, so that he fell from side to side. "You see how weak he is," she added in a low voice to Lucy.

"Yes, I see," the girl answered, and looking at Mr Lawrence she added, "We must get some power back into those legs, mustn't we? Massage and exercise."

She gave him an encouraging parting smile, not professional this time, but from the heart, acknowledging his distress and promising, proclaiming, her intention to relieve it. At the gate to which Mrs Lawrence wheeled him to make their dual farewells Lucy saw that tears had begun to cloud the despairing eyes.

2

THE GROUP PRACTICE to which Lucy Summers was attached for her domiciliary visits had its surgery in Field Road, a misnamed thoroughfare on the west side of Meadowfield, at one time existing on the outskirts of the best residential district. Now, in that district's decline, Field Road was surrounded, even hidden, by tall office blocks with shops at their feet, garages with filling pumps between the blocks, even one small factory, evil-smelling, but not particularly noisy, except when the workers arrived in the morning, dispersed and reassembled at midday and left finally at six in the evening.

The doctors in the surgery objected to the smell, but were not worried by the noise, since their working hours did not clash with those of the factory. On the contrary they assisted the practice because many of the factory hands, who had chronic complaints or recurring diseases, found it very convenient to have their personal doctors so near to their place of work that they could drop in and see them during the morning factory tea break, which coincided with the morning surgery, or at the start of the evening surgery. Since this habit did away with a substantial number of panic calls and the consequent emergency visits, usually fruitless, the doctors welcomed it. Although, in its way, it was an added exploitation of their service, it did hold a good deal of real medical interest as well as convenience and guaranteed supervision of a few difficult cases. Dr MacMann, the senior partner of the four, with his special interest in chest complaints, was particularly pleased with the arrangement and often congratulated himself and his colleagues upon building their group surgery in Field Road, several years before an old manor house opposite was demolished and its outbuildings replaced by the present works.

Lucy Summers drove her small car into the surgery carpark on Saturday morning of the week in which she had made the acquaintance of old Mr Lawrence. She had seen him for the second time on Friday of that week, the day before this, in fact.

She felt miserably confused. It showed plainly in her face as the practice receptionist, a brisk well-trained secretary, brought her to Dr Harris, breaking the order of the waiting queue.

"Miss Summers particularly wants a word with you, doctor," she announced. "She has a rather special problem. Can she — ?"

"By all means."

Geoff Harris, drearily sorting, for the N.H.S. folder, the numerous reports about his last consultation, one of those unfortunates afflicted with more than one dangerous condition, jumped up willingly.

"Bring her in," he ordered. Lucy Summers, he remembered, the girl with the brown curls and the karate grip. Brought new life to poor old Smithers, who had given up his exercises as hopeless but was now boasting he'd soon be back on the job. Well, a job of some sort. Lucy would have to tell him what sort of job he could persuade Smithers to go for.

"Good morning, Miss Summers," he greeted her as she went into his room. "About a patient? Not Smithers again, I hope?"

"No, Dr Harris. About old Mr Lawrence."

"Lawrence?" He thought furiously, unproductively.

16

"The Old Farmhouse. In Lawn Road. Just beyond all that new building on the London Road."

"Yes, of course. Hemiplegia. Lost his speech. Looked after by a rather nice daughter. That him?"

"Daughter-in-law," Lucy said. "Yes, that's the old man I mean. I'm not at all sure she's nice."

"Why not?"

His manner, his ready interest, were encouraging, Lucy thought. She wondered if his patience would match them. She struggled on, giving him the full story of her two encounters with Mr Lawrence; the first alone, outside in the garden and two days later, indoors, in the persistent presence of Mrs Lawrence.

"So what?" Geoff asked carefully when she stopped speaking.

"So I don't quite know what to think. That first morning I was so startled and so — so sorry for him, so sure he was really and truly starving — "

"Starving?"

"Yes. Literally, really *starving*! In want of food! I can't describe it."

"You've described it very well. You make me shiver."

"Now you're laughing at me, Dr Harris." Lucy got up briskly, pulling her jacket straight.

Geoff was on his feet.

"No. No, honestly. Sit down again, Miss Summers. You haven't told me about the second visit. You say Mrs Lawrence was polite when she found you with him in the garden, but was also very angry. What was she like the second time?"

"Butter wouldn't melt. Far too obvious, I thought."

Geoff smiled. Mrs Lawrence must have got the better of the physio that time, having lost out in the garden. But did that mean anything? Did any of it mean anything?

"I expect I'm exaggerating the whole case," Lucy said, agreeing aloud with his unspoken comment, which shook him slightly. "But I can't forget the sight of that poor old crippled man snatching at the crumbs the birds dropped and then later on cramming my choc bars into his mouth, paper and all."

"No," Geoff agreed, quite serious again. "Only two possibilities, aren't there? Either the old boy's nuts or he isn't getting enough to eat."

Lucy nodded.

"I know. Dr Harris, I can't go on treating this case until I *do* know which? Can I?"

This appeal to Geoff made him lift his house phone to ask if the District Nurse was still in the building. After a short pause a knock at his door brought her into his room.

Nurse Moore was an old friend of the Group. Rather slow in her work she made up for it in her ready common sense. Her opinion was always worth the doctors' attention. The question was, did she know the case?

"Mr Lawrence? At The Old Farmhouse? Yes, I have met him."

"You mean you've been there to attend him?"

"Once or twice. Not regularly. Only if Nurse Parfit can't do the morning. It's a daily visit. Personal wash and dress and bed made-up. They send out all the linen."

"Recently? Have you been recently?"

"The week before last."

"Notice anything special about him?"

"Well, no, Dr Harris. Should I? He's very thin, of course. Skin and bone. Always has been, Mrs Lawrence says. No appetite at all since he had his stroke."

Seeing the sudden interest and increase of attention in her listeners' eyes Nurse Moore was startled into saying, "What is this? Have I dropped a brick of some sort?"

Geoff smiled at her.

"I'll tell you," he said. "Miss Summers here is attending Mr Lawrence for general physio, especially to try to get him back on his feet a bit. She has a problem."

He proceeded to describe it. Nurse Moore was shocked.

"They think a lot of Mrs Lawrence at the Home," she said gravely.

She meant the Nurses Home where she lived. In addition to the General District Nurses it housed the few domiciliary midwives still attending women in their own houses instead of in hospital.

Dr Harris considered.

"Mrs Lawrence agrees that her father-in-law is too thin, even for a sick old man, but says he has no appetite."

"That's right."

"That first day in the garden he was ravenous," said Lucy.

"Mrs Lawrence could be mistaken about his appetite," suggested Geoff. "She could be underfeeding him, but not deliberately, with evil intent."

"God forbid!" said Nurse Moore, but whether she spoke on behalf of a malignant guardian or a helpless victim, it was impossible to guess.

"Well," said Geoff who knew that the waiting room held much work for him to do, "Thank you both for your reports. I'll visit the old boy myself this week. Keep on with the good work, Miss Summers, but don't try to slip him any eats. And nurse, if you could manage to do another routine for Nurse Parfit and suggest an extra mid-morning cuppa — ? Test the reaction on Mrs Lawrence as well as on the patient?"

"I see what you mean," said Nurse Moore doubtfully, foreseeing unpleasantness as well as experiment.

"I'm sure you do," Dr Harris told her, as he guided both his auxiliaries out of the room.

When he had finished the morning surgery an hour later and discussed his more complicated cases over coffee with his colleagues before they all set out on their rounds, he went back to his room. The final decision about Mr Lawrence was that he should, after visiting the patient, recommend a domiciliary visit by a consultant psychiatrist with a view not only to getting an opinion upon Mr Lawrence's mental state, but the acquisition of a speech therapist recommended by the consultant, if appropriate.

"It sounds a bit too obvious," Dr Foster had said, apologetically. "But if the poor old chap could say even 'yes' and 'no' to straight questions about his food and we could believe him — "

The others laughed. Bill Foster was the most surgically minded of the four partners, with an inborn dislike of the 'trickcyclist' angle in medicine.

Geoff Harris rang up Dr Fairclough, junior consultant psychiatrist to his own old London teaching hospital. He was lucky enough to find him in and luckier still to make him interested in Mr Lawrence. They arranged a date for a visit two weeks later, which would give Geoff time to bring himself wholly up to date with the case.

During the two weeks that passed before Dr Fairclough's visit Nurse Moore attended twice at The Old Farmhouse. On the first occasion she arrived rather earlier than she was expected, to find Mrs Lawrence, neat as usual, but in a flowered overall instead of her usual trousers and shirt. She came to the front door with a half-filled cup of coffee in her hand and covered her obvious annoyance with an artificial laugh.

Nurse Moore apologised.

"I'm too early!" she exclaimed. "I'm sorry, but I'm standing in for Nurse Parfit as well as my own list."

"Not to worry," Mrs Lawrence said, her expression softening. "Give us a miss altogether if you like. I can manage for one day, I should be able to by now."

"Of course you must do nothing of the kind," Nurse Moore said, beginning to move from the dark hall towards the downstairs room where she had last found the old man.

"You remember the way," Mrs Lawrence exclaimed, more amiably still. "Do you remember where the downstairs cloaks is, too? Then I'll leave you to it."

She reached past Nurse Moore to open a door on the right, ushering the nurse through it before closing it after her.

Mr Lawrence was in bed, half reclining against an untidy heap of pillows, but with his head thrust forward. His wheelchair stood beside the bed on one side. On the other side there was a bed-table turned outward. There was nothing on the table.

Nurse Moorse went up to the bed and put down her bag beside it.

"Good morning, Mr Lawrence," she said pleasantly. "It's me again. Do you remember?"

The old eyes regarded her carefully for several seconds, then he nodded his head.

"I thought you would." She pointed at the table. "No breakfast? Or have you finished it?"

This time he shook his head at once, several times and went on shaking it at short intervals. Nurse left the room and found her way to the kitchen. Mrs Lawrence was still there, still drinking coffee and now smoking a cigarette as well.

"Sorry to bother you," Nurse Moore said, "but Mr Lawrence can't tell me if he's had his breakfast yet or not. He just shakes his head which can mean several things."

"In his case," Mrs Lawrence said coldly, "it means he won't be ready for it until after you've done your bit for him. Right?"

"I think," Nurse Moore decided aloud, "as I'm a bit rushed for time, I'll take it in and help him with it as we go along. What does he have? Coffee or tea? Toast and marmalade?"

Mrs Lawrence stubbed out her cigarette so fiercely that Nurse Moore could not help thinking that the gesture with a knife instead of paper-clothed tobacco, might well be intended for herself or her patient or both.

Mrs Lawrence got to her feet. Her reluctance was plain

21

but she kept her temper from any further expression of her anger. She filled a small cup with lukewarm coffee from the pot on the kitchen table, scraped butter on half a round of tired brown toast from a rack that had already satisfied her own needs and as thinly spread it with jam.

"Don't bother to find a tray," said Nurse Moore cheerfully. "I can manage. He won't take long with this lot while I get my things arranged. Is this all the breakfast he usually has?"

A flash of renewed anger shone in the other's eyes.

"Mr Lawrence usually refuses to eat at all in the morning," she said harshly. "I told you Nurse Parfit gives him his coffee when she has her own. *After* his wash. When she's got him up in his chair."

"Then I hope he won't refuse to take it from me," Nurse Moore said, very calm and matter-of-fact. Mrs Lawrence stared, but said no more.

The slow process of investigation and assessment took its course. Geoff Harris found the old man emaciated, feeble and impossible to question either about his health or his circumstances. The nods and shakes of the head were too vague and far too frequent. Besides, Mrs Lawrence was present the whole time, attentive, polite, grateful for the doctor's interest and kindness. Geoff was quite impressed.

"You can't fault her," he said to Nurse Moore, comparing impressions. "He's much too thin, of course, and she quite agrees, but says she can't get him to take much. He hates not being able to eat tidily as he used to do before the stroke."

"She says that, does she?" Nurse Moore reflected. "Well, it could be so, I suppose."

In her own mind she had her doubts. A long experience of these chronically brain-damaged old people led her to expect very little from them. The character was changed, the personality blurred, not only the lost use of certain faculties. They weren't going to get Mr Lawrence improved by their therapies, speech- or physio- or whatever. She was ready to bet on it.

Hearing these views from the District Nurse, Lucy felt discouraged. But later on, after two more attendances at The Old Farmhouse, she began to wonder what she was really worrying about. Mrs Lawrence always seemed to be sitting with the old man when she arrived and if they were in the garden, always began to wheel him towards the house before she was even inside the gate. Heard and recognised the car engine by now, of course. Dr Harris had called and seemed to have fallen for Mrs L. That made her feel a fool, especially hearing all the doubtful gags about her patient's lack of appetite, relayed by Geoff, as she called him to herself, with a kindly quizzical smile, as one discounting a scare-monger.

But beneath it all the first horror, the first stark conclusion still struck at her heart when she let herself recall the sunlit corner of the garden and the bird-table and the snatched, gobbled crumbs.

He must be starving, she had cried out then in her mind. So now again, remembering. And again. And again.

The nightmare would not go away.

3

DR FAIRCLOUGH WAS a serious-minded young man, who had made psychiatry his speciality from a genuine regard for his fellowman's distress in the more obscure, but very widespread, area of mental illness. He had not travelled so far along this ill-charted road that he had lost his enthusiasm or sunk in the morasses of sentimental fantasy or crude cynicism that lay along it. Domiciliary visits did not often come his way. This request from Geoff Harris, whom he remembered as a particularly hard-headed and down to earth student, was extremely welcome. He was determined to be helpful.

This was not going to be easy. In the first place his work depended almost entirely upon speech, on exchange, deep and detailed, with the mind of the patient. He had ways of promoting an exchange with the very reticent, the inhibited, and hallucinated, the senile, the deficient, but not with the totally dumb, not with a mind that had no words available in any form, spoken or written.

He explained this difficulty to Mrs Lawrence at some length. She seemed to be a very intelligent woman and she, at least, was able to express her thoughts, though he found her in some degree insensitive in her attitude to her father-in-law. But of course that was natural and usual in those who had to live with the afflicted.

"Dr Harris wants me to try to assess the chance of Mr Lawrence recovering some power of speech," he said.

"I'm afraid from what he tells me that chance is not likely to be great, but I understand that so far Mr Lawrence has not had much professional help. Speech therapy, for instance?"

"In hospital he did," Mrs Lawrence said. "But it only bothered him."

"In what way?"

"Excitement. Bad temper." She paused and went on sadly. "He was never a good-tempered man, doctor. Very critical. Finding fault.".

"Did you see much of him then, before his stroke? I mean, you didn't live in the same house, did you? But the same town?"

"Oh no, no." Mrs Lawrence had gone a little pale. She didn't like her old father-in-law, Fairclough decided. "Not the same. But Jim took me to visit him quite often."

"So he was perhaps more than usually frustrated by his loss of speech?"

"Yes. Furiously angry, sometimes. He still is. That's why, I think —"

"Yes?"

She drew a deep breath.

"He refuses his food — quite often."

"From anyone?" Dr Fairclough was watching her closely. He realised there was conflict of a high order going on before him. The handsome face was still smooth, but rigid with another kind of anger that he did not understand.

"From anyone?" he asked again, very gently. "I mean is it personal because you have never been very close and he resents his present dependance, or simply childish because his brain and therefore his understanding have been so damaged?"

"How should I know?" she burst out, coarsely, loudly, very unlike her former quiet speech. Then at once she apologised and added, "One of the district nurses got him to take his breakfast when she came early one day."

"But Nurse Parfit can't manage him?"

25

This shook her. This fuss about his food had spread, had it?

Dr Fairclough made another mental note, seeing her confusion and coming to his own conclusion about the cause.

When he left The Old Farmhouse half an hour later he had not learned much more. Old Mr Lawrence was indeed emaciated. He was also irritable, dribbled a good deal, waved his left hand about, shook his head repeatedly up and down or from side to side in agreement or denial, but in so confused a manner that his answers, even to very simple questions, were far from clear.

Dr Fairclough spoke to Mrs Lawrence again before he left. "He is dreadfully frustrated, poor old man," he told her, "as you know very well. He is also very undernourished. This refusal of food is a common senile trait, but with him age is very much mixed up with the gross cerebral damage. I'm afraid we can't expect much real improvement in any direction, but I think speech therapy might encourage and soothe him a little. He would feel we were all trying to help him, wouldn't he?"

She nodded her head, apparently much moved by his words, though he saw there were no tears in the eyes she raised to him. "Thank you, doctor." she said gravely as they shook hands. She watched him drive away before she went back into the house to telephone the latest news to Jim.

Two mornings later Mrs Chandler, chief administrative officer of Social Services in Meadowfield, found Dr Fairclough's request form on the top of the pile on her desk. Her personal secretary, Beryl, pointed it out to her; the address on the note attached to the form was that of the London teaching hospital where he did most of his work, but there was a private address as well, in discreet small letters on the right-hand side.

Mrs Chandler read the note. She was not accustomed to this sort of thing. She rather disliked it, for it meant that this was a specialist case and she abhorred specialist cases.

26

She had set up, in less than two years, a most refined, smooth-running organisation, with an over-all workload five times the size of her predecessor's. With six times the number of helpers, of course. The cases to which she directed these variously-trained or totally untrained young men and women, nearly always fitted naturally into the slots she had ready for them. Occasionally it was not a good fit, in which case the patient, very rarely the slot, was manipulated to fit.

"Why Dr Fairclough, Beryl?" she asked her secretary.

"Dr Harris called him in for a domiciliary," answered Beryl. "It says so on the form."

"I am aware of that," said Mrs Chandler coldly. "But why not our own consultant?"

Beryl wanted to say, "How do I know? Ask Geoff Harris why not", but she was afraid of Mrs Chandler and this was her first job, which she dared not lose. She answered meekly, "Dr Harris is fairly new to Meadowfield, isn't he, Mrs Chandler?"

"He's been here long enough to know better. Anyway, we've only got one speech therapist and she's doing full-time at the hospital. Didn't this Mr Lawrence have her when he was in? I seem to remember — "

"Shall I get the file?" Beryl asked eagerly.

Mrs Chandler considered. She spent quite three minutes considering, during which time she dragged up her memories of the Lawrence pair — no — trio, wasn't it? Old father the invalid, son and son's wife, wasn't it? She had helped them to get the old boy into the geriatric ward during the removal to The Old Farmhouse. A few weeks after his stroke in another part of the country. Directly the move was over, they'd had him home. Or she had. Mrs Chandler did not remember ever seeing the husband.

"Yes, please, Beryl," she said at last. Speech therapy. There ought to be a note about that among the hospital reports.

27

There was. It did not help, since every tested result was negative. In general health the old man had gradually improved, though his walking was poor. He still could not speak at all.

Mrs Chandler read Dr Fairclough's note again. She found a sentence that gave her what she sought.

"Here we are!" she said, turning to Beryl. "He actually puts it in words."

"What's that, Mrs Chandler?"

" 'The block that holds back his speech may have a psychological origin.' Barmy, in other words. We'll send him Miss Carr. Those new people I tried her with won't have her back. She's been sorting her notes this last week. Time she went to another field job. See if she can make anything of Mr Lawrence."

Miss Carr was small and dark with a pinched little face that had not changed much since her early childhood and would stay about the same for the next thirty years. People wishing to be kind to her had called her 'knowing' when she was very young. Later they were less inclined to use an adjective of such doubtful worth. For Molly Carr did poorly at school in all those subjects where exact knowledge was essential. Her wayward mind floated uncertainly hither and thither without any particular direction. Her imagination was lively; she produced a few remarkable infant drawings and paintings. Later on one or two poems in entirely free verse astonished her teachers by the striking misuse of some long words they did not expect her to know and in some cases had themselves to look up in the dictionary. Possibly it was this collection of insubstantial artistic triumphs that won her a place in a minor college where she elected to pursue Social Studies. The result was a diploma and further training. Miss Carr continued to enjoy meeting vague, large ideas. She continued to be incapable of observing or learning any single detail of exact knowledge about anything.

But the diploma secured her a job. Having passed

through several spheres of activity where her deficiency appeared to be much greater than her worth, she discovered a final interest in the great, heaving, clouded sea of human psychology. Another course, another diploma and Miss Carr, as a psychiatric social worker, was ready to paddle about in the shallow waters of that ocean where Dr Fairclough took his lifecraft on its desperate ventures.

Miss Carr rang the bell at The Old Farmhouse and waited. She had not wanted this assignment. She had not thanked Mrs Chandler for giving her this client. "See what you can make of the poor old gentleman," Mrs Chandler had said. Lost his speech and the consultant thought it was psychological. Did that mean it wasn't a stroke? They might have told her a bit more about the case. But she couldn't get it from Mr Lawrence if he couldn't talk. His daughter, then?

As no one answered the bell she very reluctantly rang it again. Her last client had been a near-delinquent girl. It was the mother in that case who had proved impossible. Everything she had done to get the girl's confidence had been wrecked by the mother. Only wanted the poor kid put away; hospital or jail, she couldn't care less. In the end she had had to give it up. There had been complaints; very hurtful, very dangerous. It wouldn't do to fail again.

There was a faint noise inside the house. Miss Carr braced herself. The door opened.

"I have come — " Miss Carr said at the same time that Mrs Lawrence said "Yes?" on a high, enquiring note.

The two women stared at each other: Mrs Lawrence got in the next word before Miss Carr recovered and thus established her ascendancy.

"Yes?" she said again, more quietly.

"I have come to see a Mr Lawrence," said Miss Carr, "I am from the Social Services Regional Office in response to a request from Dr Fairclough, through Dr Harris."

She was quite surprised at herself for managing such a long and clear explanation without even stopping for breath. It was really her way of fending off Mrs Lawrence, whom she found frightening. It beat down her near panic. She even felt quite proud of herself.

"The speech therapist," said Mrs Lawrence, opening the front door wider. "Come in, Miss — "

"Carr," said Molly, stepping forward. She would have to explain her true position. Speech therapist, indeed! "Perhaps I could have a word with you first before I see my client," she suggested.

"By all means," said Mrs Lawrence, casually. "Come into the lounge."

The lounge, Miss Carr thought, would have been a lovely room if the furniture had not been so shabby. This hint of poverty moved her to pity. As always her imagination took wing, carrying to supersonic heights her sympathy with the devoted young couple caring for their difficult old relative.

"I must explain myself," she said. "I am not really a speech therapist."

"Oh?" Mrs Lawrence's eyes grew wary and her face stiffened a little, but Miss Carr's thoughts were within, searching for words to describe her true intention and she noticed no change.

The explanation went on for some time. When it ended Mrs Lawrence was little the wiser, but she was able to conclude that Miss Carr's intervention was unlikely to make any difference whatever to the patient. On the other hand —

"I quite understand," she said. "Dr Fairclough came to assess the permanent mental damage. He talked about frustration through not being able to speak."

"Naturally that must be very severe," Miss Carr agreed.

"But he kept hinting that the damage was not physical — "

"Psychological," Miss Carr interrupted. "That's why Mrs Chandler chose me — "

"Mental," said Mrs Lawrence firmly. "He really can't

take in a lot of what you say to him. Dr Fairclough gave me to understand he was no longer really in his right mind."

Miss Carr was daunted. A speechless client, who could not answer her questions and did not even understand them. What sort of approach could she possibly make? She said, hesitating, "Perhaps I'd better see him now, Mrs Lawrence. Dr Fairclough's report did mention the psychological angle."

Mrs Lawrence got up.

"I'll just see if he's all right," she said. "Nurse has been, but sometimes — "

Miss Carr did not see the look of weary suffering on the other's face before she left the room. She was away for several minutes. When she came back she was carrying a small tray with two cups of steaming coffee on it.

"He's asleep," she said, with a wan smile. "One of his catnaps. You never know when — But if you have your coffee now before you see him — "

"How kind," said Miss Carr, accepting the coffee with relish.

As she drank it she listened to Mrs Lawrence explaining the course of her father-in-law's illness, the reasons for their return to his old home and Jim's enforced absence on business for long stretches of time.

Miss Carr was so fascinated by this recital that she did not notice the time until her cup was empty. But when she did look at her watch she exclaimed in alarm.

"I have to go!" she cried. "And I haven't seen him yet. Whatever will Mrs Chandler say!"

"Your boss?" suggested Mrs Lawrence softly.

"The organiser, Social Services." She looked at her watch again, desperately wishing she had read it wrongly. "I really must see Mr Lawrence for a second or else — "

"He doesn't like to be roused when he's asleep." Mrs Lawrence warned. "He can be quite nasty. Surely your Mrs Chandler will understand if you say he was asleep.

31

When will you call again, Miss Carr? If I know the date and the time I will guarantee to have him awake and ready to meet you. Wouldn't that be much better than disturbing him today?"

"Yes, it would."

Miss Carr got out her diary and made a firm date, feeling the importance of her authority in so doing. Then she left The Old Farmhouse and drove away in her little car to the next client on her list, a mother of six who had not fully recovered from the birth of the last infant and was in danger of neglecting it.

At The Old Farmhouse Mrs Lawrence went to the back door to take a look at the old man, whose wheelchair was parked close at hand, no longer in the corner by the bird-table. The back of the chair was towards the door but she could see that he was exercising his left leg and arm as the physio had taught him to do. She turned away and went indoors again.

4

WHEN DR HARRIS received a written report from the psychiatrist about old Mr Lawrence he laid it before his partners. They were meeting, as usual, for coffee after the morning session at the practice surgery in Field Road. It was the second time he had put this difficult case before them. As junior partner of only six months standing he had found himself allocated a very dull section of the National Health patients. He was not replacing a retired partner, but had been taken on because the practice was expanding. So those who had joined his list had consented to do so either because they were very seldom ill and did not mind who they saw for their minor ailments, or else because they expected that a new younger man would be more up to date than the others and more inclined to listen to their recurrent, self-absorbing troubles. Consequently Geoff Harris had found his list largely made up of chronic cases, the elderly, the neurotic, and medical disasters such as Mr Lawrence.

"Why this man Fairclough?" asked the senior partner, Dr McMann.

Geoff explained the connection. The others nodded.

"Very cagey, naturally," Dr Bingham said, referring to the report. "Doesn't say if he found the old chap barmy or not."

"He suggests speech therapy," Geoff pointed out. "So he must think that might help."

"Help him to diagnose the case or help the patient?" asked Dr Foster.

"Both, I suppose."

"I wonder." Dr McMann considered and then asked, "Didn't you tell us a week or two back there was something odd about his diet? Some report by an auxiliary? Physio? O.T.?"

"Miss Summers," Geoff said and repeated the strange story the girl had told him. His colleagues shrugged in total disbelief.

"Who has he got for speech therapy?" Dr Bingham asked after a pause. "I thought there wasn't one available around here."

"A Miss Carr, Mrs Chandler said."

"*Carr!*" Dr Bingham was outraged. "That bloody little bitch! No damn good to anyone! Psychiatric social worker, my foot! Halfway round the bend herself!"

"Calm down, Tom," McMann soothed him. "She did no harm in the end. In fact throwing her out on her arse did Miss Price a power of good. No more threats of suicide, were there?"

Dr Bingham grinned. One of his most cherished private patients, a retired headmistress, to whom he charged minimal fees, was recovering from a relapse into depression and this satisfying state was mainly due to her bout with Miss Carr and her triumph in their final shocking encounter on her doorstep, with the psychiatric social worker flat on her back on the pavement.

The four doctors dispersed on this ironic note. Geoff Harris marked up another visit to Mr Lawrence in his diary and went off to see if Nurse Moore was still on the premises.

He found the District Nurse assembling her small batch of freshly-sterilised instruments. Lucy Summers was with her.

"Ah," Geoff said, briskly. "Caught you both gossiping, have I?"

"By no means," Lucy said, defending herself. Dr Harris, she knew, could not be more than three years older than herself. He was the least formidable of the four partners, he had already shown sympathy with Mr Lawrence's predicament. "We were talking about Mr Lawrence," she went on, but stopped, because Dr Harris had turned to Nurse Moore and was asking, quite seriously now, "Well, nurse, was the poor old boy really starving?"

"I couldn't be definite as to that, doctor," the nurse answered. "His daughter —"

"In-law," Lucy put in.

"Yes, daughter-in-law, if that makes any difference. Well, she hardly left me alone with him at all. I had to push her out when — well, to save the patient being embarrassed. Apparently she's never been like that with Nurse Parfit."

"Is it significant?" Geoff asked.

"It might be," Lucy said. "She was certainly furious when I talked to him the first time, when she was out and he ate — "

"Yes," Geoff interrupted, to stop a repetition of the story his partners so clearly repudiated.

Nurse Moore said steadily, "Mr Lawrence is very emaciated, very weak. He can tell you nothing. He answered questions by nodding or shaking his head. Questions about his food make him very agitated, but Mrs Lawrence has a full explanation. He won't let her help him with his meals. She tries very hard because she realises he is not eating enough."

"Sounds reasonable," Geoff muttered.

But Lucy said, with feeling, "He would have gobbled up anything I gave him that first morning. It was horrible. I know he was starving! I know he isn't crackers!"

Geoff smiled at her kindly. She was pretty and she had a good figure; well built, obviously strong, but not as hefty as some of the physios. And observant, too.

"Does Mrs Lawrence stick around with you, as well?" he asked.

"Not now. But she doesn't give me coffee and biscuits like she does Nurse Parfit and the social worker."

Geoff raised an eyebrow at Nurse Moore.

"Yes, I've spoken to Parfit," Nurse Moore said. "Asked her to try giving Mr Lawrence a biscuit with his coffee. He does get some of that now. Since you made your visit, doctor, and discussed his food."

"I see." Geoff turned away. "Well, I must get going. Carry on the good work, Miss Summers. If he can't eat or talk at least you can try to get him more mobile. On his feet or by working his wheelchair himself. Does he know how, or is he far too weak to manage the brake and get it moving?"

"I'm not sure," Lucy answered. It was certainly an idea. She added gratefully, "I'll try. It could help him a lot, couldn't it?"

"Might put up the morale," Geoff said as he turned away.

It was three days before he found time to make another visit to The Old Farmhouse. It was raining, so the patient was in his chair near the front window. He seemed to be alone, staring out, no expression on his thin, lined face. But when Geoff lifted a hand to him in greeting he dragged up his shaky left hand from his lap and waved it excitedly, while a wide smile showed his instant recognition of the visitor.

No serious mental impairment, Geoff thought, then remembered the overriding damage and tried to assess how much of the real, original Mr Lawrence had survived the stroke. He had reached no definite conclusion when Mrs Lawrence, in a neat flowered apron and wiping her hands on it, opened the door to him. As Geoff had intended she had clearly come from the kitchen and the final stages of preparing the midday meal.

"I do apologise," he said in his best professional manner, "but I got held up over an emergency."

"Mr Lawrence is not in urgent need," she said stiffly. "In fact he has not changed at all since you were here last."

Geoff took a careful step forward, forcing Mrs Lawrence to give way. As he continued to advance she retreated, until at the door of the room where Mr Lawrence was, he stopped and stretched for the door handle.

"He isn't —" she began, but Geoff smiled at her and said, "He waved to me as I reached the front door. Nothing really wrong with his brain, I'm sure. Only this loss of speech makes him seem peculiar."

Mrs Lawrence had gone very white. She grasped the door handle, pushing aside Geoff's hand. She burst into the room before him and stopped short so that he, following, nearly collided with her. Over her head he saw Mr Lawrence in his wheelchair in the centre of the room, facing the door.

"You said — " Mrs Lawrence was now scarlet with rage. "You couldn't — "

But Geoff was already beside the old man, greeting him, explaining why he had arrived at an inconvenient time, that he need not examine him.

"Dr Harris knows we are just ready for our dinner," Mrs Lawrence said, controlling herself. "He can't stop."

Geoff congratulated himself again on his timing.

"But I can help," he said. "And it will give me some idea of your main trouble over his food. Perhaps you would fetch his meal, Mrs Lawrence, if it is ready and I will see how he manages." He turned away, almost propelling her to the door, speaking in a low voice. "Nurse Moore tells me she had no difficulty getting him to eat his biscuit when she had coffee with him the time she came to attend him. I'll see if he takes the meal from me."

Mrs Lawrence gave in. She brought a plate of cottage pie and peas; a small helping indeed but nicely cooked, served in a soup plate with a spoon and fork. Geoff took it from her at the door.

"If you don't mind I'll give it to him myself," he said. "We want to get to the bottom of this psychological hitch, don't we? I'm sure you understand."

She stared at him and he smiled back at her.

"I won't let him throw it about," he said.

She forced herself to smile back and went away.

Mr Lawrence was so excited when he saw the cottage pie that his hand shook too much to take the spoon. Geoff had to feed him. The little helping disappeared in no time at all.

"That went down all right," Geoff said when the plate was empty. "Want some more?"

Mr Lawrence's head nodded up and down several times.

"Why don't you take it from your daughter-in-law?" Geoff asked.

This time the head was still, but tears gathered in the old eyes and began to run down from them.

"Look," said Geoff. "I think you aren't eating enough, so we'll have to make some other arrangement. It may be you could have a few weeks in hospital or perhaps meals-on-wheels would help Mrs Lawrence, spare her some of the cooking and so on. If I get a different scheme working, will you help by eating properly?"

"Yes," Mr Lawrence said, quite clearly and distinctly.

They stared at each other. Geoff was the more startled of the two. He picked up the plate, spoon and fork.

"I'll see what I can do," he said. "I'll come back in a week or so, unless you're in hospital by then. I'm sure a change of diet would help you."

This time Mr Lawrence's answer was only a sob and more tears flowed.

Geoff reported his success to Mrs Lawrence in the kitchen. He noticed that she had laid a place for herself on the table there, with a fair-sized cottage pie of which only a small helping was missing.

"He'd have managed a bigger helping," he told the silent woman. "We'll have to build him up, you know."

He explained his ideas and to jolt some reaction from Mrs Lawrence other than her obvious resentment he added, "He was quite agreeable. He actually said 'Yes' to my ideas."

"He did *what*?"

Clearly this had roused her. Her answer was shrill; she was not only angry, but frightened.

"They do react like this sometimes," he explained, though his wisdom came only from the reading-up he had done on Mr Lawrence's type of aphasia. "Didn't realise what he'd done. No guarantee it'll lead to anything."

"He might get his speech back?" she said, with something like horror.

Geoff looked at her with cold eyes.

"Wouldn't you like that? We did call in Dr Fairclough for a real purpose. To see if he thought it possible that Miss Carr — "

"Miss Carr, my fanny!" said Mrs Lawrence coarsely. "Fat lot of speech training he gets from that young lady. If you ask me she doesn't know the first thing about it!"

Geoff looked at his watch. He had spent far too long with Mr Lawrence, though in some ways it had been valuable, most valuable. But he doubted if his partners would agree with him.

"I must go," he said, disregarding Mrs Lawrence's last remarks. "I'll try to give you a break from looking after him. I know it can be most wearing, but we are trying to help. You, as well as Mr Lawrence. Incidentally, is your husband expecting to be away much longer? Abroad, did you say?"

"Spain. I don't really know. His business — "

"Quite. But I think he ought to see his father as soon as possible, because he has deteriorated in the last six weeks and you never know with these cases. The basic condition

39

of his heart and arteries is the same, you know, and won't change."

"I understand, doctor."

She saw him to the door. It was still raining. She saw the doctor wave a hand before he walked off towards the gate, so she waited until he drove away before going into the front room.

Mr Lawrence in his wheelchair was back near the window, staring out. He did not move: did not seem to have heard her. She closed the door again softly and went back to her cooling cottage pie. But her appetite had gone: she felt too upset to eat, she told herself. So she pushed the pie away and made herself a pot of strong coffee instead.

Later that day, after six o'clock, she dialled a long number. The answer came almost at once, far sooner than it could have done from Spain or indeed anywhere outside the British Isles. She broke into rapid speech and continued for several minutes. She knew she must make the situation clear at once or Jim would do nothing but ask questions and that always confused her and then he was angry.

Jim was very angry now. He called her a lot of rude names. He said she was a bloody useless cow, she had got herself into a right mess and she could fucking well get herself out of it without him. She reminded him that it already looked bad his never coming to Meadowfield. He told her, with embellishments, to go to hell and rang off.

Sobbing, Mrs Lawrence concluded that Jim had found yet another bit of comfort in his business endeavours. If it did not solve her present problems, he might leave her. Just when she had looked like bringing off a winner.

She sat by the telephone, smoking cigarettes and cursing her luck for nearly an hour before she cleared up the kitchen and then watched television until Nurse Read, the evening attendant, came to put Mr Lawrence to bed. By that time she had worked herself into such a state of desperate misery that she was ready to confide in the first person she met. Unfortunately this was not Nurse Moore nor even Nurse Parfit, each of whom knew a good deal about the case and about the circumstances at The Old Farmhouse. Nurse Read, on the other hand, was new to this particular job and had no great liking for geriatrics.

So she listened with impatience to the long confused story that Mrs Lawrence poured out to her: she managed to bring it to an end by demanding hot water and basins to get on with her job, and having attended to Mr Lawrence swiftly and efficiently she avoided hearing a renewal of his daughter-in-law's woes by walking firmly out of the house, after giving the complainer a short, direct piece of advice.

"Have a talk with the Social Services, dear," she told her. "You need to get the right help for this case."

"I'm getting too much help," Mrs Lawrence burst out in desperation. "All different. I'm at my wit's end."

"Mrs Chandler will sort you out," Nurse Read said, moving rapidly away towards the gate.

"Bloody bitch!" Mrs Lawrence said aloud, but too softly for the insult to reach its target.

However, she took the advice. She booked an interview with Mrs Chandler herself, a privilege not everyone was able to achieve. She only had to wait forty minutes before she was shown into the Area Administrator's office and asked to sit down.

Mrs Chandler listened sympathetically, making a few notes. These took the form of hieroglyphics or more simply 'doodles', because Mrs Chandler knew that the computer, already fed with all the various reports on the case, had made its own assessment for her.

"There is trouble over his food, then?" Mrs Chandler said, breaking into the recital.

"I never complained," Mrs Lawrence answered. "It was the doctors."

"There is a suggestion of returning him to hospital?"

41

"I wouldn't mind, but he's well enough. As well as he ever will be, I'd say."

"But he doesn't make any progress, physically or mentally, with his speech or walking?"

"I don't trust that Miss Summers — "

"The O.T.s have their own control."

"She's the physio."

"So do most of the domiciliary ones. Have their own control."

"As for Miss Carr — "

"Well?"

"She's supposed to give speech therapy."

Mrs Chandler frowned.

"She's supposed to make a psychological assessment. I have no available speech therapist at present."

"I thought the consultant, Dr Fairclough, did that. The assessment, I mean. Dr Harris as much as said so."

"We have had reports from both doctors," Mrs Chandler said, smoothly. Which did not add anything to the argument.

The two women looked at one another. Mrs Chandler prepared to sum up the situation in the Lawrence home and wipe the slate clean. In both these activities she had always shown the brilliance that had brought her to her present position.

"I think," she said, "that everything has been done and is being done that can be done. But it is all getting to be too much for you, Mrs Lawrence. I think, if your husband can afford it, a holiday by the sea for you and the old gentleman would make the sort of break for you both that might help you to settle down again later with your—er—burden."

She rang a bell on her desk. Beryl came at once. Mrs Chandler gave an order. The girl went away and came back with a ten-page printed pamphlet.

"This gives you a list of suitable holiday homes and

42

lodgings where you could take Mr Lawrence. If you get fixed up and will let us know where you are going, we will arrange the ambulances and so on for the journey."

She got up to show Mrs Lawrence out.

"I do hope you will benefit," she said, with a kind but vague smile.

As the carefully groomed figure of her client disappeared she turned to the girl beside her.

"Beryl," she said. "Make a note that Mrs Lawrence is taking the right steps."

"Yes, Mrs Chandler," her personal secretary said, meekly.

Mrs Lawrence did arrange a holiday at the small town of Seacombe on the South Coast. She was determined that it should benefit herself, Mr Lawrence too, one way or another.

Thinking over her visit to the Social Services office she blamed herself for not going there before. It had been altogether too easy. Perhaps she ought to have realised this, seeing that the ghastly Miss Carr came from there. But never mind. Going on this holiday she'd be able to drop all those busy-body women now clustered round that old obstacle in his wheelchair, who continued to obstruct her path. Drop them, turn them off, the doctors with them, and never have them back.

All thanks to Mrs Chandler. Violet Chandler she was down as, in the brochure on 'Holiday Homes for Invalids'.

Violet looked like doing her a bit of good. She'd certainly latch on to Violet. Tell Jim? No, send him a card from Seacombe. Or a promenade snap. Herself in a bikini? She laughed soundlessly as she stared at herself that evening in her bathroom mirror.

5

HAPPENING AS IT did in the early days of the holiday season and at a weekend, the fatality, the tragic accident as it was universally described, found a place in the national as well as the local papers. More journalists than usual were prowling the seaside resorts, watching for stories, however familiar, however hackneyed, that they could work up into drama or pathos, or even horror. The death by drowning of a crippled old gentleman confined to his wheelchair, was a novelty no editor could refuse to print.

In Meadowfield Lucy Summers and Geoff Harris, among many others, recognised the names and the face of the principal figure, though Mrs Lawrence did not appear among the photographs. Nurse Moore, at work at the partnership surgery, was the first to remark upon it to Geoff.

"So our poor old Mr Lawrence has gone, doctor," she said, passing Geoff as he opened the door of his personal consulting room, carrying a number of patients' record cards in his hand.

"Best thing that could have happened to him," said Geoff, who foresaw a long session that morning and wanted to get on with it.

"Not that way," said Nurse Moore stiffly. "I wonder whose fault it was his wheelchair went over into the sea."

"I expect we shall know after the inquest," said Geoff briefly, escaping into his room.

Unfeeling young brute, he couldn't care less, thought Nurse Moore, looking into the waiting room to call out the first 'dressings' case she was there to attend.

But Geoff was not unfeeling, only too busy with the living to give any thought just then to the dead. He cared, too, a great deal, because he had not been able to impress upon his partners the serious predicament he found himself in over old Mr Lawrence. He wished he had been able to fix a bed for the old boy in a geriatric ward before the poker-faced Mrs Lawrence had whisked him away to the seaside. He knew most of the arrangements had been made, always at the taxpayers' expense, by the Social Services. Was it some local seaside do-gooder or busybody who had let the wheelchair slip off the pier? Or was it Mrs Lawrence, whom he had been almost ready to think might be underfeeding her ancient father-in-law on purpose, as Lucy Summers believed? Oh hell, he thought, it's going to nag if I don't find out a bit more about it. Perhaps Lucy — ?

The girl herself felt even more deeply, for with her, regret was sharpened by guilt. She had very deliberately worked on Mr Lawrence to make him more mobile, not only by encouraging him to walk, in which he had not made much progress, but in manipulating his wheelchair with his left hand and arm.

This had not been easy. The brakes on the chair were near the front of the wheels, one on each side, but they were not easy to reach by someone as old and shaky as Mr Lawrence. He had learned fairly quickly to find the knob on the left side and push it over. Later he had managed to reach down to find the knob and pull it up. But the right-hand brake was more difficult. His right hand and arm were quite useless; he could not twist his body so as to use the good left arm and hand. But Lucy made him an angled stick with which he could at least release the brake, though not pull it up again.

She had not told Mrs Lawrence about the old man's

45

progress, but she hoped he had used it, when he was left alone in the garden, to move himself into and out of the shade on a hot sunny day. Perhaps to move under the cherry tree where the fruit had already set, though it would be dangerous for him to try to pick it or later to eat it unripe.

Dangerous and yet she had known how desperate he had been for food when she had gone first to The Old Farmhouse. Had he been desperate again at the seaside, so much so that he had decided to end his life by pushing off the brakes and waiting for the holiday crowds to give his chair the push that would start him on his way to final peace?

When Geoff saw her later in the day travelling in her Mini as he left a patient's house he waved an imperious arm to her to stop, which she did a few yards further along the road. But she did not get out, just sat waiting for him to reach her window. He saw a pale troubled face, no smile, clouded eyes. He guessed the reason and said, "Mr Lawrence? Yes, I feel bad, too. I ought to have done more — got him into hospital, where they'd have fed him enough, even if it was monotonous."

"I ought to have done less," Lucy said. "It may have been my fault." She explained why.

"Rubbish!" Geoff said sharply. "You aren't seriously suggesting it was suicide and you put him up to it?"

Lucy began to cry.

"Oh hell!" Geoff said. "Must you? Look, we ought to get this thing straightened out as far as we can. We can't go on having secret thoughts of foul play versus senile decay, can we? Nor can we go on about it all, here and now. Have dinner with me tonight, can you? Meet me at the surgery, seven thirty. O.K.?"

"Yes," said Lucy. "Thanks."

She was surprised to find her tears now quite irrelevant, her state of mind restored to normal working. She even wondered where Geoff would take her for the meal.

It was a modest restaurant not far from the flat which she shared with a friend who worked in a bank. She had often passed the place and had even sometimes read the menu, but had considered the prices too high for her present salary. Besides, Sue liked cooking and had regular hours of work.

"You know this place?" Geoff asked, watching her face as they went in.

"Only from the outside," she answered, smiling.

"I come here a good deal," he told her. "It's not at all bad."

He did not explain why he ate out 'a good deal', but Lucy knew that he was not married and now concluded that he did not live with relations either. Geoff, in fact, lived at present with a recently married sister in a house at the far end of Meadowfield. Vaguely he felt he ought to find himself a separate establishment and in the meantime spent as little time as possible in this temporary home. He paid for his keep, which helped his brother-in-law, but did nothing, he knew, to make him more welcome.

On this particular evening he was totally preoccupied with the unexpected death of old Mr Lawrence. As soon as he found a table for Lucy and himself and had ordered the usual traditional English dinner, he asked again the question that had started Lucy's tears.

"I'm sure we ought to compare notes about Mr Lawrence," he began. "You mustn't be upset," he added, quickly, so quickly that Lucy laughed gently.

"I'm all right now," she answered. "It was just the shock earlier today. And knowing that I had taught him to get the brakes off his wheelchair and put them on again on the left side, his left side, I mean. He could knock off the right-hand brake, but he could only pull up the left hand one."

"So he might have taken an opportunity on purpose to drown himself? Not really very likely, do you honestly think?"

47

"I don't know." Lucy had thought of nothing else since the morning, but she said slowly. "I really haven't had time to make up my mind. Not really thought about it."

And that's a lie, Geoff thought, a real whopper.

"Honestly," he said. "This food business. What have we got? Your own impression on your first visit. That he was ravenously hungry."

"I'm certain of that," Lucy declared.

"Taken as proved, what else have we got? Mrs Lawrence junior's story that he wouldn't let her help him over his food, or your impression that she was deliberately withholding it, starving him, in fact?"

"I think she wanted to get rid of him," Lucy insisted. "With the help of the nurses we found he would eat everything they fetched for him themselves."

"He ate for me, too," Geoff said. "It was a ridiculously small helping, as a matter of fact. I ought to have got him into hospital straight away."

"Could you have?"

"Not easy. He wasn't an emergency — not really — not physically."

"He was skin and bone. I know she didn't want him to go to hospital. She told me she was so grateful to Mrs Chandler for suggesting the seaside. It was sure to give him an appetite."

"Horrible!" Geoff made an angry noise. "Ugh! The Chandler bitch again! Her people had been round to badger old Lawrence several times. I tried to warn them off, but it didn't work. There was a Miss Carr — "

Lucy nodded.

"Psychiatric social worker. No good at all for speech therapy."

"So that's what she was. Fairclough asked for speech therapy. I wonder if he knows what Mrs Chandler was up to?"

Frustrated and angry Geoff and Lucy parted outside the restaurant. Their mutual indignation had brought them to such a point of contact that each regarded the other as at least an ally, at best an understanding friend. Not that they had decided upon any definite action. How could they? Neither was in a position to do so. Besides, with the patient dead, action of any kind was pointless. He had gone, his troubles were over. In the dreary, old-fashioned, smug phrase, it was 'a happy release'.

Not, however, just yet for Mrs Chandler. Dr Fairclough was enraged. He had tried to telephone Mrs Chandler, only to find she was 'in conference' with other administrators and the girl at the exchange could not tell him when she would be free. He repeated his name and standing and the urgency of his need to speak to Mrs Chandler. The answer showed indifference amounting to gross rudeness.

Dr Fairclough rearranged his work to give himself a couple of hours free in the early afternoon and drove to the Meadowfield office of the Area Health and Social Services. He demanded to see Mrs Chandler at once, or failing her, her deputy. There was stubborn opposition at first, but it crumbled when he turned from the reception desk to make a direct assault upon a door marked PRIVATE, at the end of a passage.

Mrs Chandler, white-faced at the intrusion, did not find her voice until Dr Fairclough had stated the object of his brisk appearance, ending with the words, "The girl who took my call this morning refused to put me through to you on the grounds that you were in conference, whatever that may mean. She was bloody impertinent. If that sounds too strong, I'm sorry. But I've had to waste my time making this personal visit."

Mrs Chandler said faintly, "Can I help you?"

It was the phrase she had used for many years in all the positions she had held as she climbed the steep administrative ladder of the Social Services. She uttered it now in her desperate need to dispose of this angry man. Later she would be perfectly fluent in dealing with those who had failed to protect her from this shocking intrusion.

"I doubt it," said Fairclough bitterly. "Nothing can help my patient now. He's dead, as of course you know, if you've heard the news today. And you, I understand, aided and abetted his daughter-in-law in taking him away from Dr Harris's care."

Mrs Chandler rallied.

"That is a most extraordinary thing to say, Dr Fairclough. I simply suggested to poor Mrs Lawrence that a change of air might help her in her very difficult circumstances. I suggested Seacombe as we have very satisfactory accounts of it for convalescents."

"Mr Lawrence was not convalescent. The damage to his brain was permanent. Dr Harris wanted to have him back in hospital for a food problem. Mrs Lawrence took *your* advice instead. Gross interference. I asked you to provide speech therapy and you sent a thoroughly incompetent, badly trained psychology worker, a Miss Carr. Why?"

"Because I had no speech therapist available," said Mrs Chandler, more boldly.

"Then why not report that?"

"I sent Miss Carr to make an assessment of the case."

"*I made an assessment!*" roared Dr Fairclough. He saw Mrs Chandler sway forward and controlled himself with an effort. "Don't you understand," he went on in a calmer voice, "it is for the medical profession to diagnose and treat sick people, not, I repeat *not*, for this mass of unqualified, so-called helpers, well-intentioned though they may be."

"Miss Carr has been fully trained," said Mrs Chandler faintly. "We understood from her assess — from her report, that poor Mrs Lawrence was in need of relief. Such a nice client," she added.

"We were not treating *Mrs* Lawrence," Fairclough answered, rising from his chair. "Mr Lawrence was directly in the care of Dr Harris. I examined him upon his speech disability and the mental damage he had suffered due to his hemiplegia. I ordered speech therapy and agreed that

50

the patient was suffering from malnutrition. That will be my evidence if I am asked to give it at the inquest. Good afternoon to you."

Not waiting for an answer he stalked to the door and without looking back he went out, ignoring several young women in the reception area and one elderly man at the front door, who tried, half-heartedly, to bar his way and ask questions.

They heard me shout at her, Dr Fairclough told himself ruefully as he climbed into his car. He knew quite well that he was inclined to get emotional about his choice of profession. He had decided long ago that he had a perfectly serious, objective interest in psychiatry; that he was not halfway round the bend himself, as he considered at least half his seniors to be. But he knew too that any derogatory remark about, or implied attitude towards, his professional standing was liable to make him blow his top. Oh well, it might be a good thing to send in a complaint about Miss Carr's activities, or lack of them. But not, of course, to Mrs Chandler. To her next in eminence, her boss, whoever that might be. As for the inquest, time would show, but probably nothing much.

When she was alone, after this most unpleasant, searing, almost dangerous interview, Mrs Chandler lit a cigarette with trembling hands and sat back in her chair to recover and reflect.

She then picked up her house telephone receiver and said in a faint but composed voice, "Margery?"

"Yes, Mrs Chandler," the office exchange answered.

"I want to contact Miss Elaine Brigg of Seacombe. I think you have the number."

"Yes, Mrs Chandler. At once."

"Put her straight through to my office."

"Yes, Mrs Chandler."

The call came very quickly. Also there was no need of explanation.

"I was expecting to hear from you, Vi," Miss Brigg was

saying in a high excited voice as Mrs Chandler leaned forward to rub out the last half inch of her cigarette. "It's about that poor woman, Mrs Dorothy Lawrence, isn't it?"

"Yes, Elaine. I suppose you have been in touch? I told her to contact you for nursing as soon as she got to Seacombe."

"She did, indeed. I told her you and I had trained together and that you had given me the outlines of her case. Of course it is not quite three weeks since they arrived. She is pathetically upset."

"I'm sure. Will you be at the inquest?"

"Oh yes, I think so. Will you?"

"I hope it won't be necessary. My plate is always very full here. Besides, the doctors are difficult, jealous of their position, you know. Prejudiced."

"Bad luck. They eat out of our hands here."

"How do you manage that?"

"Well, because the hotels find them a lot of private practice among the rich visitors in the season, foreigners largely, with sunburn and tummy bugs and so on. They don't reckon to be bothered with N.H. geriatrics, except for emergencies. They get those through the police as a rule or direct from the hotel managers."

"Which is how our Mr Lawrence's accident got into the papers, I suppose?"

"Well, yes. But she, his daughter, rang us at once."

"Daughter-in-law, not daughter. Has the son been sent for? In Spain, I understand."

"So she told me. I haven't seen him yet."

Nor had anyone else. An inquest was opened, though there had been no response to a B.B.C. S.O.S. message broadcast several times and repeated by request in Spain. The verdict was death by misadventure.

Mrs Lawrence did not appear in the coroner's court. A medical certificate, excusing her on grounds of shock, was presented by Miss Elaine Brigg, head of the Seacombe

Social Services department. The manager of the guest house identified the corpse; the local pathologist gave the cause of death as drowning and confirmed the other medical evidence of gross disability. The pier manager described the shocking accident, when the invalid chair ran forward through the crowd, the people automatically making way for it, without realising what was happening, Mrs Lawrence failing to get through in time and the chair falling into the sea just as the ferry began to swing in alongside. The seamen were intent upon taking the ropes flung to the pier from the ship. They did not see the chair until too late, though one of them dived in after it, risking death or injury from the screw, as the captain of the ferry swung his vessel away again.

The press found the case in court disappointing. The main questions from the coroner related to the state of the pier rather than that of the victim. Also to the rules for controlling the crowds and the routine observed when the barriers were removed to allow berthing the frequent ferries.

Lucy found the account very unsatisfactory, especially as Geoff seemed to have lost interest in the whole case. But the next time they met at the surgery he stopped and said, "I hope you don't mind, but I'm going to the police here and now. If you don't want to join me, say so."

"But I do!" Lucy said, delighted. "I didn't say anything yesterday because I thought you were fed up with the whole thing."

"Far from it."

"But will the police *do* anything? The verdict was misadventure. How could anyone prove now that it wasn't?"

She was right, of course. The police Detective Inspector who listened to their story pointed this out to them very conclusively. He also said, "Even if Mrs Lawrence had been trying to starve the old gentleman to death quietly — a very nasty idea as he couldn't speak out to tell anyone — she wasn't very likely to push him off the pier, attracting

53

maximum publicity to herself, was she? She had to get his chair into position where the railing had been taken down temporarily. There were notices and a roped barrier. As well as the big crowd waiting to go on the boat when it berthed."

"Yes. A lot of people milling about all looking out to sea at the ferry and up to the sky to where the advertising aeroplane was telling them what to go to that evening."

"Granted. And he knew how to work his chair, you say, Miss Summers?"

"Yes," she answered miserably. "It could have been suicide really, couldn't it?"

"I doubt it," said the Detective Inspector, bringing the interview to an end.

But he reported the conversation to his Chief Inspector, who found the young people's suspicions far-fetched, but Mrs Lawrence's dislike of Lucy Summers disturbing.

"If Mrs Lawrence wanted the old chap dead it was pretty natural, I'd say. But to plan to starve him, if true, was vicious, though safe from her point of view. To keep on hating the girl who was teaching the old man useful tricks with his chair is very unreasonable now he's dead. Unless Miss Summers knows or Mrs L thinks she knows, something vital."

"Apart from the old boy's death, or even her treatment of him?"

"That's the idea." The Chief Inspecor nodded. "What do we know about the Lawrence family? The Old Farmhouse belonged to them quite a time. Still does, though this old one and his son have never lived there, or not in my time. Why not see how long? And who inherits it? This son, presumably? Still in Spain? Odd he hasn't turned up yet? Never been seen in Meadowfield and even now, with his father dead in an accident, not a sight or smell of him. Nor at Seacombe either!"

54

6

THE CONTINUED ABSENCE of Mr Lawrence junior seemed to both Geoff and Lucy to be more than odd. That of his wife, too, until Geoff heard from Mrs Chandler that the funeral was to take place at Seacombe.

"We learn from the Area Chief Social Services Officer there," Mrs Chandler said, "that until her husband takes over the estate poor Mrs Lawrence is very short of funds. They are helping her to the best of their ability, but that does not warrant transferring the body to Meadowfield."

"I don't believe for a moment Mrs Lawrence is all that hard up," Geoff said when he had reported this interview to Lucy. "The Old Farmhouse wasn't being run on a poverty basis, that's for sure."

"Of course not," Lucy agreed. "Nor her clothes, nor the larder, according to Nurse Moore, though she was there only once or twice."

They thought it over.

"Incidentally," Geoff said at last, "the old boy never did actually farm here, did he? Or even come back to live here until after his stroke."

"You mean he wasn't much known here? But he must have had a branch of his bank and therefore a bank manager."

"Perhaps even a solicitor."

"I suppose so. But how do we start to find all that out? And is it worth it now?"

"I'm still curious," Geoff confessed.

Part of their problem was solved for them by the weekly *Meadowfield Advertiser*, which in addition to its declared purpose of exchange and mart, set out in ten pages, also gave three pages of local news, chiefly stories that had appeared in the national press about local characters. Mr Lawrence's death plunge into the sea was considered to belong to this category. An unusual local cripple suffering a violent death could not be passed over. Besides, the Meadowfield editor was a practising Christian and lived in the neighbourhood of The Old Farmhouse. He thought he remembered seeing a series of plaques on the wall of his church bearing the name of Lawrence. He verified this fact and brought it into a short paragraph in his paper.

Lucy Summers, too, had heard of the plaques. Her flat mate, Sue Collings, who also attended the church, though at very irregular intervals, took her there. They found the memorials, three in number. The first had been set up for a Jaspar Lawrence, yeoman, who died in 1743: it commemorated also his wife and children, numbering ten, of whom two only appeared to have survived their infancy. The second plaque was put up for a James Lawrence, perhaps a son, but more probably a grandson, who died in 1814. The third leapt a still wider gap, but mentioned three generations, the last James having died in battle in the First World War, leaving a wife, a son and two daughters.

"All the boys called James or Jaspar," said Sue. "Do you know which name your old chap had?"

"Not really. But the son, Mrs Lawrence's husband, must be James. She mentioned him once or twice, but she called him Jim."

"Same thing."

"So my Mr Lawrence would have been Jaspar."

The two girls turned away from the wall of the church nave, to which the plaques were fastened.

"All those Lawrences must have lived in Meadowfield

56

and been fairly important," Lucy said thoughtfully as they left the church. "I wonder why my Mr Lawrence went away and never came back until a month ago. I wonder when he left."

"And his son, too. Did you ever see him?"

"Oh, no. He's been abroad all the time. On business in Spain, she said."

After a pause Lucy went on, "I suppose they really are the same family of Lawrences? I mean as the ones on the plaques?"

"Why not have a look at the registers?" Sue suggested. "Births, deaths and marriages."

"Oh, yes," Lucy agreed. "Of course. Where? Does the church have them?"

"Marriages, christenings, funerals." Sue was not exactly sure. "There's the public registrar's office, too," she said doubtfully, then added, "I'll ask Mr Gilman. That's our vicar. He's always helpful."

Mr Gilman was more than helpful, he was interested. This led him to greater activity than he might otherwise have displayed. In a very few days he invited Sue to bring her friend to the vestry one evening. He showed them the register in several volumes laid out in line.

There was no doubt that Lucy's Mr Lawrence was the direct descendant of the farmers who had owned The Old Farmhouse since at least the middle of the seventeenth century. Also that the name of the eldest son in each generation was alternatively Jaspar and James. Lucy was able to confirm that her patient had been Jaspar and therefore his son was James.

"But there is no entry for the latest James here," Mr Gilman said. "Perhaps he was born elsewhere or not christened. You can check the birth with the civil register."

"Of course," Lucy nodded. "But Jaspar did get married here, didn't he?"

"Born here in 1905, so ten years old when his father was killed on the Somme. You can check that on the War

57

Memorial list in the Lady Chapel, 1915, the Somme. Jaspar was thirty when he was married in this church in 1935."

"So the widow and Jaspar stayed in Meadowfield until 1935 anyway. But we don't know when Jasper's son was born, do we?"

The vicar shook his head.

"Jaspar must have been in the Second World War then, unless he was reserved as a food producer," Sue said. "But that need not have been here. We still don't know where he was after his marriage or where his son was born."

Mr Gilman nodded gravely. He felt he had done his bit rather well in helping these girls, but he was not prepared to engage in competitive speculation.

Lucy understood this. She thanked him, checked quickly her notes of the more important dates and drew Sue away to find and inspect the War Memorial.

"Just one more suggestion," Mr Gilman offered, following them. "I was talking to one of the assistants of the estate agents, Johnson and Stone, yesterday and I mentioned The Old Farmhouse and he told me his firm had had the letting of the house for a great many years until it fell vacant about two years ago. He was very surprised when the Lawrences came back and shocked old Mr Lawrence should be so ill and so afflicted and now gone in such a tragic manner. The old home and so on. Very sensitive young man, I thought."

The girls thanked him again for all his kind help.

"I bet the house agent was worried whether young Lawrence would sell The Old Farmhouse without the help of Johnson and Stone," Geoff Harris said when Lucy repeated the clergyman's words to him. "It's odd," he went on, "that he hasn't turned up in Meadowfield yet. Lawrence, I mean."

"Probably at Seacombe with Mrs L coping with the funeral. They'll come back together, I suppose."

But this was not so, for only Mrs Lawrence made her appearance a week later, turning up one morning at her former dairy to start the delivery of milk, at the newsagent next door to order her newspapers and the *Radio Times*, and at the bus stop with her shopping bag to visit the centre of Meadowfield with its big stores, banks and other essential services.

Among these the estate agents Johnson and Stone were relieved to see her arrive and not surprised by her visit. She took their condolences very calmly: there was mutual agreement over 'a happy release' and 'an end to suffering'.

The young assistant spoke of shock; Mrs Lawrence described 'wonderful understanding and help'. A Miss Brigg, who directed the Social Services in that area, actually knew their own Mrs Chandler. This had given her a feeling of added support. The inquest — well, it was called misadventure. She did not want to talk about it. She was going to join her husband and they wanted to sell The Old Farmhouse. Would Johnson and Stone put it on the market? They would like to get rid of it as soon as possible.

Johnson and Stone would be pleased to accept the commission, the young assistant said. Would Mrs Lawrence give him an address where they could find her? Mrs Lawrence said of course, she would write to them. At present she was packing, while waiting to hear from Mr Lawrence when and where she should join him.

This vagueness a little surprised Mr Stone, now the head of the firm and to whom his young assistant had related the interview with Mrs Lawrence.

"No address?" he said, severely. "Why not?"

The assistant again suggested shock.

"Rubbish!" his boss replied. "Mrs Lawrence doesn't know the meaning of the word. I saw her come in from my office window."

This rebuke led the assistant to look up the file relating to The Old Farmhouse. He was surprised and pleased to find that the papers covered a great many years. Earlier letters signed Jaspar D. Lawrence succeeded a very old yellow one about the fencing off and sale of a parcel of land signed by James F. Lawrence in 1912. It had been written to S. Johnson, who had retired from the firm after fifty years spent in running it.

The young assistant was suitably impressed. Also he had letters from the newly defunct Jaspar Lawrence, relating to the farmhouse, written at intervals of several years until the latest one from an address near Penrith, announcing an immediate return to Meadowfield. This was followed by one from Mrs Lawrence, signed Dorothy Lawrence, from an address in Lincoln, dated a month later than that. He took the whole file to Mr Stone.

"Right," the latter said. "We must wait till she gives us fuller instructions. No need to move till she does."

"She said to put the house on the market."

"So you told me. What does she want for it?"

The assistant reddened.

"She didn't say."

"You mean you didn't ask her?"

"I thought — "

"She was suffering from shock. Look. I'm not going to the expense of getting out a description, which means a detailed visit by appointment, photographs, measurements, the lot, when the property may not even belong to her husband. It can't belong to her, can it? And where is he? This son, James. Looks like a very long-standing family row to me. Don't you think so? Is there a will? Have they a local solicitor? Why make his wife do all the dirty work? Abroad? Business? Even now, with his old man dead?"

The assistant was far too confused by this tetchy harangue to have any thoughts at all, beyond those of immediate escape from the boss's room. But he told the whole story of his interview to his young wife and she told it to Mrs

Gilman at the Women's Institute meeting two days later and she in her turn repeated it to the vicar who happened to see Lucy Summers outside the house of a sick woman they were both visiting.

"But of course I knew they came here from Lincoln," Geoff said when Lucy passed the news to him. "It was the Lincoln Hospital report that came to us with him. He was only in our hospital here two days as a very special concession while the move was on."

"So Lincoln Hospital would have the Lawrences' full address in Lincoln," said Lucy.

"Of course."

Geoff left her then but he looked for her the next day at the end of the group practice's morning surgery.

"I've been thinking about what you told me," he said. "Lincoln seems to be very little more than fifty miles from here. What do you say to taking a day off to look up the chap who wrote to me about old Lawrence? A good letter, quite human for a cagey consultant."

"Fine," said Lucy, wondering how to manage a day's leave in mid week.

"I'm due for a free weekend the one after next," Geoff said, putting an end to her uncertainty.

"Will we be able to talk to the people we want to see at a weekend?" she asked.

"Have to. We're pretty busy in the practice just now. I couldn't get away earlier."

"O.K. then," she said, trying to sound both casual and willing, though really she was quite excited.

The hospital consultant who had written to him was away, Geoff found, but the registrar was welcoming and helpful. He was glad to meet someone in general practice, he said, because he was getting fed up with the general chaos in hospital life just now and was thinking of giving up his former aim of consultant for a calmer, more purely medical existence as a family doctor. "My own old man was one," he confided.

"Same here," said Geoff.

"You don't have to ask the people who clean your surgery how you may treat your patients? Or whether they pay fees or not, I hope?"

"Christ, no!" said Geoff with feeling. "What I want to ask you is have you got the address in Lincoln from which Mr Lawrence was admitted? And the details of the onset of his hemiplegia?"

"Sure," said the registrar.

Geoff was able to copy the notes direct from the ward file and then, still in the record office, to take down the address he sought.

This turned out to be a guest house in a rather run-down, formerly genteel part of the city. The owner or manageress who opened the door to them herself, was at first suspicious.

"Not the press again?" she asked, across the door chain she had not unfastened.

"No, indeed," said Lucy, who was to be the spokesman for this visit. "But about Mr Lawrence, who was a patient of mine for physiotherapy. At Meadowfield," she added.

"Come in, then," was the cautious answer. Evidently there was some real interest here, some wish for fuller enlightenment.

This soon became plain. The old man and the lady with him had been in her house only two days when he had his stroke, poor old gentleman. The other gentleman had roused her early, about six in the morning, asking her to get a doctor, or ring for an ambulance. His father, he said, had fallen out of bed, seemed to be partially para-lysed and half conscious. She had called a doctor who had called the ambulance. He had gone straight off to hospital.

"Where he stayed for just on a month," Geoff told her, "before going to The Old Farmhouse at Meadowfield, which was his old home."

"So the old gentleman told me," the landlady said. "Wanted Mrs Lawrence to see it. They intended to be with

62

me about a week for the old place to be got ready for them. I knew that from his letter."

Lucy and Geoff exchanged glances.

"Would that be the letter engaging the rooms here?" she asked.

"Why yes. Would you like to see it?"

"Please." Geoff suppressed his eagerness. "You see, as his doctor in Meadowfield I am looking now for a really complete picture of his illness and what went before the stroke. So if I could — "

The manageress had already left the room they were in, still talking as she went. It was clearly a communal sitting room, though there did not seem to be any other inmates about.

"Shall we get the address they came from?" Lucy whispered.

"That's the idea. Shush!" The manageress was back, with a folded piece of writing paper. It began 'Dear Mrs Smith' and was signed Jaspar M. Lawrence.

When they had both read it Geoff said gravely, "Mrs Smith, I wonder if it would be too much to ask you if I might keep this letter? For research purposes, of course."

"Research?" Mrs Smith was understandably surprised.

"The writing," Geoff explained. "To compare — I shall be in touch with his own doctor, of course, in — near Penrith, is it? The onset of disease — any evidence of change — "

"Well," Mrs Smith was impressed by the range of enquiry the young doctor was suggesting. "Of course young Mrs Lawrence settled with me fully. She stayed on, naturally, until she could take him to Meadowfield. She had a power of attorney by then, of course. I don't really know why I kept his letter, except I was sorry for him, being struck dumb like that."

"Just so," said Geoff, putting the letter into his wallet. "I'm sure we're very much obliged to you. Mrs Lawrence paid your account, you say? Not her husband?"

"No. He — Oh, I see what you mean. No, Jim came for the day really. The second day they were here. Old Mr Lawrence booked two single bedrooms. Young Mr Lawrence had not intended to stop, because he was due to go abroad next day, but in the end he did and shared with his wife, of course. Lucky he did, with the old gentleman taken ill so suddenly."

"Very lucky," said Geoff. "Well, thank you for all your help. We must be getting back to Meadowfield."

"Odd," Lucy said, after they had been on the road for half an hour, Lincoln now far behind.

"Which bit, particularly?"

"That old Dad booked the rooms and young daughter-in-law paid. This son of his gets more and more dubious the more we hear of him. Jim, the landlady called him. That's odd, too."

"Very," said Geoff. "Nearly always abroad, never much in control, it seems. I'm not sure I like our Mrs Lawrence."

"To put it mildly," said Lucy. "Have we ever? Liked her, I mean. But such a pet of the Social Services. What's the betting she had them under her thumb in the north, the poor clots? If she and Jim were living on Dad then, as later?"

"We may have the means now to discover," said Geoff, taking a hand off the wheel to pat his inside wallet pocket.

7

ANOTHER WEEK PASSED. Mrs Lawrence, still apparently alone in The Old Farmhouse, went quietly in and out, usually taking a mid-morning bus to the town centre. Her neighbours in Lawn Road watched her passage from their windows or their front gardens. They were still feeling a vicarious satisfaction over the publicity given to Mr Lawrence's fatal accident. True, journalists no longer haunted Lawn Road. But they were remembered. They had brought with them 'a piece of the living past' as they called it; erroneously, seeing that the press at that time was concerned only with the dead present. But this activity roused in many a curiosity about the Lawrence family that persisted, though the local paper's attention had been diverted by a mild explosion in the boiler room of the town baths. This had coincided confusingly with an unseasonable thunderstorm. The two loud bangs destroying the peace of the early hours made a fresh memorable occasion.

But those of the neighbours who had elderly relatives in the town were very willing to fish in the weedy, stagnant waters of their memories and some could even dredge up a few ancient stories about the Mrs Lawrence who kept the farm going with the help of a manager while she brought up her son and two daughters, deprived of their father by the First World War. In a roundabout way the gist of those tales reached Mr Stone of Johnson and Stone, handed to him by his wife when she revived the subject of The Old Farmhouse one evening.

"It's going to be sold, isn't it?" she asked. "That's what I've heard."

"Who from?"

"Mrs Lawrence, the young one, gives it out, I gather, whenever she's asked."

"I'm sure she does. Wants us to sell it for her."

"Don't you want to?"

"Yes, when I know who owns it."

Mrs Stone considered this.

"You mean young Mr Lawrence hasn't come to Meadowfield yet?"

"Nor he wasn't in Seacombe at the inquest, nor even at the funeral. Very odd, with air travel so easy."

"Spain, she says apparently. Urgent business for his firm. I wonder what prevented him."

Mr Stone laughed.

"Driving under the influence? Pushing drugs? Knifed, trying to make the client's wife?"

"Really!" Mrs Stone said, trying to control her own mirth. "You are awful! The Lawrences are an old family and a very respectable one. Old Mr Lawrence's mother, as I've just told you, kept the farm on till he married and then they gave it up and he went off with his wife to be near her cousins in the north and then — "

"His mother must have joined them and he wrote to us to let it for private use and sell the farmland and out-buildings. Which we did."

"Where exactly did he go?"

"Between Penrith and Carlisle. Hillside Farm. Can't remember the exact name of the village, if there is one. Anyway in what they now call Cumbria."

"Farming? Hillside Farm, you said?"

"I suppose so. One of my young chaps showed interest in Mrs Lawrence when she came in to see us the other day. He looked up the file. Lawrence sometimes used

Belmore and Hobbes over the lettings. They probably know a bit more of the Lawrence history, but it's not my business. Not after the last letting anyway and that's more than two years ago. I don't know any of the other firm now, since it changed the head of it."

"That was young Mr Belmore, wasn't it?"

"Not so young when he left."

Having reached a dead end Mrs Stone could find no more questions to ask. Mr Stone was not, in any case, prepared to answer them. Time was sure to answer the only question to which he needed the answer in his business. Who was the owner of The Old Farmhouse? Was it young Mr Lawrence and if so why did he not appear?

Mrs Lawrence, of course, knew the answer, and this knowledge disturbed her very much. She had hoped to sell the house fairly easily and was both discouraged and alarmed by Mr Stone's unwillingness to proceed. She had not realised the full extent of her own ignorance in these matters.

So upset was she, indeed, that she made several telephone calls in the evenings of the next few days on long numbers that were certainly not in Spain or any other country abroad. The answers after prolonged argument, gave her very little comfort. Her Jim refused to appear in Meadowfield. Once had been enough, he said; thinking of Lincoln still gave him the heebie-jeebies.

"But that was just bad luck," she insisted.

"Which I've bloody well had a basinful of since we left — "

"I know, I know! But we've got to sell this house, haven't we? It goes to you, doesn't it?"

"Should do."

"Of course it does. I've sent the will along with a covering letter giving your address, saying you were back in England. But it would look a lot better if you were here at The Old Farmhouse."

"That's as may be, but you know damn well I can't risk it. Even Seacombe was a risk I daren't take."

"You'd have been all right at Seacombe. Why not?"

"The press. The photographers, you silly cow."

That floored her. Besides, he rang off before she had thought of an answer. More than ever she feared she now had a rival. It wouldn't surprise her, but it did add to her difficulties. Not to mention the expense. The dual account at the bank she held with her husband was still available, she was still in the black; but it was getting lower and lower, less than a hundred, she calculated. It would soon run dry and though the manager had been sympathetic, like everyone else since she came back to Meadowfield, he would naturally expect Jim to replenish it suitably.

Her thoughts went round and round. She rang up Jim again, simply to ask for money. If she had to appeal to their bank manager and he referred the problem to the Penrith people and they used the address he had given them —

"Bitch!" he snapped at her. "That really puts the lid on it. I'm not there now as you very well know. So what's the betting they write and get no answer. And the next thing is the Law gets asked to help?"

"You could send me a cheque, couldn't you?"

"On the Meadowfield account? Don't make me laugh!"

"On your personal account. I know you've got one. Always did, as well as this joint one and power of attorney."

"Mind your own bloody business!" he shouted and rang off again.

Mrs Lawrence felt a sense of deep outrage as she put down her own receiver. Coming back to The Old Farmhouse had been his idea, after all, when a month had passed in Lincoln without the old man showing any real improvement. He had chosen to disregard the obvious risks, otherwise they would not all have moved to Meadowfield. She had done everything she could to please him.

Perhaps she had always known his professed love went no deeper than honeymoon enjoyment. A short honeymoon, she told herself, turning the blade of his neglect most painfully in her wounded heart.

But presently her feeling changed to one of anger and deepened to that of a desire for revenge. She would not endure these hints of betrayal. Not now, when they were so near the inheritance. It wasn't only the house itself. It had lost the chance of big development money due to the stupid old fool's obstinate refusal to get demolition permission. It was what it would shortly be worth in compensation when the new road was built. But time was running out and so was her bank balance.

Mrs Lawrence, as she had attempted to explain to Jim, had already found her bank manager, though fully sympathetic, less than helpful. Even the ridiculous Miss Carr, so utterly incompetent, had filled in a small corner of the over all picture of anxious care she had tried so hard to present. To the Social Workers then, and this time milk them to some real purpose or her name wasn't Dorothy Lawrence.

"Show her in at once," Mrs Chandler said, quite excited to have this now famous client in her waiting room. She rose to her feet as Mrs Lawrence came in.

"My dear," she said, deepening her voice and allowing a little throb to enter it. She remembered, as she spoke, how effective this tone of voice had been in her early days, how it had secured her early promotion to her present administrative post. "I did so hope I should see you to say how very sorry I was to hear about your loss, the horror of the accident, the shock — Do sit down."

She felt she must sit down herself, so deeply was she feeling the other's misfortune. Yes, her state was genuine, as it had been in those early times in the field, genuine, wildly romantic, a welter of misapplied ideals and sketchy principles, so soon dissolving in the over-all atmosphere of competition, mixed with that heady realisation of the delights of power.

Mrs Lawrence sat down, waiting for the froth of Mrs Chandler's too rapidly drawn sympathy to settle. In the face of her client's sober calm it soon did so.

"Seacombe," said Mrs Chandler in her normal voice. "I hope Elaine Brigg was able to help and advise?"

"She was splendid," said Mrs Lawrence. "She sent a social worker round to see us the day after we arrived. Quite early, to wash and dress Mr Lawrence. She gave us the names and addresses of doctors who generally attended our guest house. Not that I needed to call one because the accident — "

"Don't talk about it if it distresses you," Mrs Chandler urged, hoping none the less to promote a flow of interesting detail.

"It helps not to bottle it up," answered Mrs Lawrence, following her original intention. "Actually there is not really very much to tell. It happened so suddenly, so unexpectedly."

"Yes. The papers gave that impression."

"The papers were not on the pier when it actually happened," said Mrs Lawrence tartly. "They came running and waving their cameras immediately afterwards, hampering the rescue and the recovery — "

She paused for breath and Mrs Chandler, touching a button on her desk, ordered coffee for two in a whisper.

Mrs Lawrence resumed her story. "I had taken Mr Lawrence on to the pier as usual. It was a fine day, with a lot of people about, particularly at the point where boats came in to take tourists for trips across the bay. I left Mr Lawrence on the opposite side of the pier, away from the bulk of the crowd. I wanted to buy a newspaper for him and cigarettes for myself from the kiosk. As I came back I could see the big launch coming along to discharge passengers and take up the next lot. There were men shouting at the crowd to stand back and I knew the ropes were being fastened across the gap where the pier railings had been slid away. Then I saw Mr Lawrence wasn't where I left him."

"How awful!" Mrs Chandler murmured. "Had someone moved him?"

"We never knew."

Mrs Lawrence's face had gone very pale and her expression as she said this showed far more anger than grief. But Mrs Chandler did not notice this. She was busy taking the full coffee cups from the girl who had brought them into the room. When she handed one of the cups to Mrs Lawrence she saw only the deep distress of her client.

"I suppose not," she murmured. "In such a crowd."

"We never knew," repeated Mrs Lawrence, "because that stupid Miss Summers had taught him how to unlock the brakes on his wheelchair. It had one on each side, to push forward to undo and pull back to fasten. He had always managed to move the left-hand one with his good arm, but the right one he couldn't manage, even to undo, until she taught him, first with a stick, then by swinging his good leg across."

"Wasn't that very dangerous?" Mrs Chandler asked, disturbed by the thought that any client might be found to show initiative, and even more outraged to discover one who had been actually taught to do so.

"Of course it was dangerous, highly dangerous," Mrs Lawrence agreed. "She said he had every right to move himself about without assistance if he could do so safely. Because not being able to speak he couldn't tell anyone where he wanted to go."

"But he couldn't always do so safely, could he, poor old gentleman? Not that he could have wanted to throw himself and his chair into the sea."

"The chair was not lost," said Mrs Lawrence. "I got to him just in time — on the brink, as you might say. If the crowd had helped instead of moving back on either side, the poor clots — "

"Oh!" said Mrs Chandler, now really horrified by this picture of dire stupidity, misunderstanding and muddle. "You mean they *made way for him,* knowing as they must have done there was no railing and only a drop to the sea. But the rope — surely the rope?"

"The rope was higher up than the chair," Mrs Lawrence explained. "About waist high, I suppose, to control the crowd and the queue for the launch. I caught hold of the handlebar of the chair and the rope saved me from being dragged over the edge too. But Mr Lawrence was tipped out into the sea."

"How awful!" Mrs Chandler said. "He couldn't hold on with his good left hand?"

"He didn't try. I always thought his mind had been affected by the stroke, not only his speech and body. But the doctors wouldn't have it."

"I know," Mrs Chandler agreed, remembering Miss Carr. "The psychiatrist wanted a speech therapist but the medical branch had no one available. The best we could do was the psychiatric social worker we sent you."

"Miss Carr, yes," Mrs Lawrence smiled gently, remembering her dealings with Miss Carr. "I'm afraid they didn't get on together at all."

"No," Mrs Chandler sighed. "I believe the medical side has recommended her for a refresher course in her subject."

"I'd have thought something in the strictly domestic line — "

"She has a degree, you know."

She was a damned ignorant little fool, Mrs Lawrence thought, and an obstinate, arrogant one as well. But she said no more about Miss Carr, only guided the conversation back to her own most urgent needs.

In the end she had what she had come for, advice upon how to approach the Social Security people, her bank manager, her husband's solicitors. And more than advice: a note setting out what services Mrs Chandler had already supplied and an appreciation of her client's worthiness for maximum help in her present difficulty.

"I am very much on your side," Mrs Chandler said warmly. "You must not feel alone in your trouble. I'm sure," she added, "when your husband comes back from Spain and his father's will is proved, everything will be all right. But his presence will, of course, be necessary."

As if I didn't know that, Mrs Lawrence thought, but aloud she thanked Mrs Chandler profoundly and went away to try her luck with those sources of income the Social Services had recommended.

She had varying success. The Meadowfield bank manager understood fully about the delays caused by wills and those who suffered thereby. He wanted to get in touch with the two Lawrence accounts in Cumbria.

"One," said Mrs Lawrence, beginning once again to feel desperate over Jim's absence. "We shared. After Jim's father had his stroke and lost his speech we had a power of attorney since he could not sign his name."

"I know," said the bank manager. "He made a mark with his left hand instead, to give his consent, because his mind was not affected."

"At Lincoln, yes. We had intended to be there for a few days only, but he was taken ill almost at once and was in hospital for a month."

"But you meant to come back to The Old Farmhouse in any case, I understood."

"Yes. To see about selling it. But when we did get here he wanted to stay."

The bank manager looked at her carefully.

"So what about your former house in Cumbria; not far from Penrith, isn't it?"

"Nearer Carlisle." Mrs Lawrence fumbled for a handkerchief. "I don't know. We — Jim — "

The bank manager was indignant. He was ready to believe any evil of this James Lawrence, who chose to pursue some vague business ends in Spain, or perhaps further abroad, instead of dealing with his father's illness and death and his own subsequent inheritance. In connection with that he remembered having a word with Stone over the proposed sale of The Old Farmhouse. Well, perhaps now he knew where to apply for detail of the Lawrence account in Cumbria, he could check on that property as well. And possibly put that branch in touch with Stone, who could not begin to act yet, of course.

"We really need old Mr Lawrence's solicitors on all this," he said, causing Mrs Lawrence to shrink and scream inwardly, though she only grew paler than before. "But in the meantime I am sure we can accommodate you for reasonable amounts. At least until your husband is able to take charge of your affairs. So please don't lose sleep on account of the petty cash. It won't be for long, will it?"

They shook hands, she thanked him cordially, with a brave little break in her voice that made him escort her to the outer door of his bank and watch her progress, which was brisk and firm, down the street.

Poor little woman, he told himself. I wonder what that hubby of hers is really up to?

He sighed.

8

MRS LAWRENCE CONTINUED to live quietly at The Old Farmhouse, upheld by the modest help her bank manager afforded her, together with some extra aid from the Social Services recommended by Mrs Chandler. And so things went on for another three weeks and the neighbours in Lawn Road, except for those who lived next door and directly opposite, began to lose interest in the lonely woman. It was taken for granted by this time that young Mr Lawrence, who had not yet made any appearance in Meadowfield, either before or since his father's death, must have deserted his wife now that she was not needed to look after the invalid.

At the end of the three weeks, on a Saturday morning, the blow fell. Mrs Lawrence's worst fears, the long dreaded outcome of events, took shape. It came in the form of a letter from a firm of solicitors, Boll, Shin and Gregg, writing from their offices in Carlisle. It was to these people that she had written, after the accident at Seacombe, explaining that Mr Lawrence's son was abroad so that she was inquiring on his behalf to ask if the deceased's will was in their care, as she had been given to understand at the time of her marriage, or if it must be looked for in the house near Penrith that they had left in May for their visit south. She wanted the will dealt with as soon as possible, so that The Old Farmhouse could be sold.

Now here was the answer. It was a very disagreeable

shock indeed. Messrs Boll, Shin and Gregg had to inform her that they held two wills drawn up and signed and witnessed by the late Mr Jaspar Lawrence. By the earlier one he had left the Cumbrian property exclusively to his son, but The Old Farmhouse to her, personally, By a later document, drawn up in Lincoln in May of that year and forwarded to them by a firm of solicitors of that town, the whole of his property, of whatever kind, was left to his son. Nothing was left directly to her.

The final blow came in the last paragraph of the letter.

'Mr Jaspar Lawrence, in a note attached to the latest will, did furnish us with his son's present address, so we were able to notify him at once upon learning from the newspapers the tragic account of his father's death. We are puzzled and surprised you have not been in touch with him. We trust you will understand — '

She understood only too well. She cursed again for the thousandth time her near-panic move in taking Mr Lawrence away from The Old Farmhouse, from those wickedly suspicious bastards who were trying to remove him from her care. Publicity: hadn't Jim always said that was the main thing to avoid? Well, why had he left everything to her, then? Who could have foreseen the old brute's cunning? No wonder he drove himself into a stroke! Lincoln, of all places!

She fought for calm and presently achieved enough to decide what ought to be done to save something from the wreck of her plans. She realised now that her thoughts had been moving in one direction only since the catastrophe on the pier at Seacombe. It looked as if Jim's mind had been travelling in the same direction. So it was more vital than ever that they should meet, discuss it, decide on their separate roles and then part. This time, for ever, she determined, setting her mind once more to search, invent, imagine, contrive, decide. And act.

The day had been fine, a continuation of the seasonal, early autumn fine weather. Her mind being now quite made up, she went into the garden. No one had done any work for her there since those spring days when the interfering Miss Summers had found Mr Lawrence near the bird-table. Her own fault for being late home? Anger rose in her again, but she suppressed it. As far off as May and now it was October. Incredible that the struggle had gone on all this time and that Jim had resisted her persistent calls to him to show himself, at least for a few days, even just a weekend.

Well, now he could not avoid it, or if he did he would realise what her own next move must be. God forbid it would be necessary. Grimly, she continued her inspection of the neglected garden, the weedy paths, the roof drains blocked with leaves, the worn rusted bars at the old cellar window, the coal-hole chute, the smelly outdoor gardener's privy.

When she had finished this tour of inspection and made a few adjustments, she went indoors to continue her work there, in the intervals of trying to contact Jim on the telephone. She succeeded at last, for her news and her argument and finally her threat brought the positive result she had waited for so much too long.

Jim would not be able to get down until after dark, say half past eight or nine. He would travel by train and walk up from the station. He rang off before she could dispute this plan, which seemed to suggest he would have no luggage with him. Perhaps that would not matter. But surely she would need a car to take away her own belongings?

Jim would need a meal. She resented the need to cook, but decided to make it a final effort, smiling to herself at the double meaning she intended to give that unwelcome chore. Before she set to work she made herself a pot of coffee and lit a cigarette. She took it into the sitting room that ran the length of the house with windows at each end, being two original rooms knocked into one. She moved to the front window and sat down near it, looking out into Lawn Road.

It was now just after six o'clock, but clouds had gathered while she was working outside the house and it was very nearly dark and distinctly threatening. A thunderstorm, she decided. Please God it'll come and go before Jim arrives. A soaking wet man in a bad temper — Jim's kind of bad temper — She stared at the house opposite, catching sight of her neighbour there, who evidently had reached the same conclusion about the weather, for she smiled, pointed at the sky, and mimed a state of fear.

"Silly old biddy!" Mrs Lawrence said aloud, which the neighbour, trying to lip-read, quite misunderstood to refer to the approach of rain, for she nodded and shrugged and moved away out of sight.

The storm broke at about the time Mrs Lawrence began to cook the dinner. It flashed and boomed for half an hour or so and then died away, only to come back in a couple of hours time with renewed force and twice as much noise in the frequent bangs. But Jim missed the first part, arriving only slightly dampened by drips from house roofs.

His temper, however, was as bad as Mrs Lawrence had feared. It was not improved by finding the whisky bottle empty and the gin bottle only half full.

"This all we've got?" he asked, shaking the gin bottle at her.

"Up here, yes," she answered, stooping to the oven.

"More in the cellar, you mean? Where's that?"

"Can't you see I'm busy? It's off the hall, on the right."

She knew he had never been in this house before. His own fault, for being so ultra cagey.

"Don't you know these old places have cellars?" she asked scornfully. "Use your loaf."

"He'd never have wanted to come here, if you'd managed him better."

"I like that. If you hadn't been so obvious. I told you he

78

smelled a rat. A hundred times I told you. But that made no difference. Oh no!"

"He was off his nut. Before as well as after!"

"He was never off his nut! Cunning old devil! Read that!"

She threw the Carlisle solicitors' letter at him so hard that it struck his face and fell to the ground. As he stooped to pick it up she saw his eyes blazing with fury. But he whitened as he read. When he had finished he laid the letter on the kitchen table and spoke in a dangerously quiet voice that made her shiver inwardly.

"I wish to God I'd never took up with you," he said. "You've made a balls up of it all along. Lincoln to begin with. I was never with you in that. Then here."

"Liar!"

"Then rushing off to the sea. Of all places — "

Her patience broke. She was taking the roast meat out of the oven. She shook the baking tin in her rage so that fat spurted up into her face.

"Liar! Liar!" she screamed, slamming down the tin and with the basting spoon flinging boiling fat at the hand he was pointing at her.

With a roar he was on his feet, one hand shaking off the burning agony, the other reaching for her neck. She ran round the table, not daring to go away from this barrier between them, picking up knives, forks, plates, glasses, to throw at him, kicking over chairs to trip him, praying that the gin she had laced with her sleeping pills would take effect in time before he caught her.

It did. He stumbled over a fallen chair and went down heavily. When he had pulled himself up his fury had melted away. Sullenly he set the chair right, gazed at his injured hand, went over to the sink and held it under the warm tap, wincing as he did so, not looking at her.

Mrs Lawrence, after standing with her hand at her side for a few seconds to recover her breath, dished up the meal and set it on the table.

"Dinner's ready," she said in her usual, calm, even voice. "You must be hungry, aren't you, Jim?"

He looked at her, amazed as always by her powers of recovery. A hell-cat one minute, an elegant iceberg the next. Perhaps it hadn't been her fault all along, but his own for not being capable of giving her up. But then that was her fault, too, wasn't it? Would he ever be free of her? Wasn't she a very long sight too risky? Hadn't he better — ?

Before he went to his prepared place at the table, which she had very quickly straightened and restored, he moved round to hers, put his arms round her and kissed her, long and hard. Even as his mouth moved on hers he was thinking, "I shall have to get rid of her soon," but he let her go and went back round the table to his place, where a full plate of attractive food was waiting for him.

He started piling it into his mouth, until Mrs Lawrence checked him with an acid remark.

"Does she starve you, then?"

He stared at her, the hate in his eyes growing until it began to frighten her. She had felt his hand on her neck tighten before he kissed, so she knew that he was more dangerous now than he had been before their enforced separation. She knew that an end, one way or another, must decide matters.

She said, "Why, we have nothing to drink with our dinner! Are you too hungry or greedy or whatever, to get us a bottle of something?"

He looked about him, then said angrily, "Where?"

"In the wine-cellar, of course. I told you."

"Which is — ?"

She made an elaborate sigh, put down her napkin, pushed back her chair.

"Of course you don't know the house, do you? Not my fault, that. I told you before you went off your rocker. Along the passage, the last door on the right. The light switch is on the left as you go in."

The storm, having circled the hollow in which Meadow-field lay, had come back over Lawn Road, more directly over it than before. The resounding crash of its first impact drowned her words. Jim, from the door, shouted to her to repeat her directions, adding, "Why don't you show me? Lazy, bloody bitch!"

"I'll show you," she said, but he was already through the door and did not hear what she said, nor the voice in which she said it. He only knew that she was staying behind, but following, until he let her pass him. Then she went in front until she stopped before the last door in the narrow passage, where she stepped back as he reached for the lock and turned the key.

"What d'you want? I mean, what have you got?"

"Any old plonk as far as I'm concerned. Take what you like!"

Again her voice was drowned by the thunder. Her neighbour, opposite, always said afterwards that you couldn't hear yourself think, let alone hear a noise of any kind from over the road.

The next day dawned bright, with the low October sun shining on the wet trees and hedges, glittering on the bent petals of late roses in the suburban gardens. Several housewives and their husbands were out on their porches, sweeping away sodden fallen leaves and invading mud. As a rule they did not speak much to one another while engaged on menial tasks, but on this occasion, and a Sunday, after a night of disturbance and anxiety, in some cases of genuine terror, they were ready to purge their unwelcome dose of crude reality with a spate of explanation.

"I really thought the glass house roof had gone," one called.

"I'm not surprised," answered another. "We had a positive waterfall in the larder. The storm window was blown right in. Not that there was any food there. That's all in the fridge or the deep freeze, of course."

They laughed over the unwonted confusion and parted to go indoors.

During the period of their conversation and during all that morning there was no movement in the porch of The Old Farmhouse, though a couple of branches from a dying elm had fallen across its roof and might even be blocking the entrance. But Mrs Lawrence did not come out to set matters right, which was unlike her, her opposite neighbour remarked in the road that afternoon. Nor did she appear on the next day, nor the next.

By this time the husbands had remarked upon the total absence of movement by day in or about The Old Farmhouse and the absence after dark of light in any of the windows. First with their wives, then in groups among the near neighbours at the pub, they were agreed upon several curious things. First that on the night of the storm Mrs Lawrence had been at home and had waved to her immediately opposite neighbour just as the lightning began to flash and the thunder to rumble in the distance.

"I did look out again once in the interval of the storm," this neighbour said. "I'm too nervous to do that while it's on, but I did then and she had her light on in the porch as if she expected someone."

"That's right," another agreed. "Someone did come. I must have looked the same time as you because I remarked upon the porch light and the gate clicked as someone opened it, but I didn't want to be caught snooping, so I dropped my curtain and I didn't see who it was went in. The porch light was out after that."

"Nobody seems to have noticed her leaving, if she's really gone," the first neighbour remarked. "I wonder if anyone did."

As the third day passed and a common interest brought the husbands to gather in the local pub for an urgent exchange of news, the strange silence at The Old Farmhouse found greatly increased attention. It became known and accepted that Mrs Lawrence had received a visitor, probably a man, from the figure's height and build, wearing jeans and an anorak, with the hood up over the head, sandals on the feet and no luggage.

"And pretty wet, soaked through, I judge," said the latest informant. "Must have been the chap you all mean. I was giving Caesar a very short run on the lead. Hates thunder, poor little brute. Didn't want to leave the house, though it was during that break in the rain. I didn't notice him go into The Old Farmhouse. Wasn't looking. Caesar needed the attention."

They were agreed then that Mrs Lawrence had indeed opened her door to a visitor. It was left to the landlord of the pub to supply a possible sequel.

"He didn't stay," he said, breaking into the conversation that he and several others had listened to with growing interest. "I looked out of the bedroom window just after the storm finally ended. It was Sunday morning by that time. You could still hear a bit of thunder now and then, but the rain had stopped. There was someone coming down Lawn Road, passing on the other side. Couldn't see much, still very dark, no street lights this end. But an anorak with the hood up. I saw that all right. Carrying a bundle or a case, I don't know which."

"Man or woman?" a voice asked.

"How do I know?" The landlord was indignant. "You can't tell the difference from the back in broad daylight, let alone on a black night at two in the morning, being kept awake by a bloody storm."

Silence followed until the landlord moved away and the Lawn Road neighbours drifted apart to find other acquaintances.

If these people felt any qualms, any genuine unease over the non-appearance of Mrs Lawrence, they must have suppressed it, for they took no steps to investigate her sudden, complete disappearance or the meaning of the arrival and later departure of her visitor, carrying nothing, it seemed, when he arrived, but burdened by a case or bundle when he left. One further note was added by a friend of the landlord, who had not been present during the discussion in the pub, but had called privately after closing time.

"Sounds like some joker on a bit of breaking and entering," he suggested.

"No breaking. She let him in, friendly, Mr Parsons said."

"Before the storm got here," the friend said, "I was in Lawn Road myself. Nearly dark, it was, and I saw what we were in for, so I was hurrying. You know or perhaps you don't, the hedge is quite high round The Old Farmhouse. You get a glimpse, just a glimpse of the garden as you pass the gate. There was a man in there, looking up at the house. Short jacket — could have been an anorak. Casing the joint, as they say, I wouldn't wonder."

"Well," the landlord told him, after reflection, "if you're so sure of that, you'd better go to the fuzz and get them to check Mrs Lawrence isn't lying in a pool of blood in her lounge, hadn't you?"

"Not likely," his friend said, laughing. "They'd want to know what I was doing myself up in the Meadowfield Game Park at that time of day, in that kind of weather."

9

On Monday morning Mr Stone's assistant came to him in a state of some excitement.

"You'll never guess, sir, who's just come into the office," he said in one rushed breath.

"Why the devil should I?" responded his boss immediately. He had not yet recovered from an unusually heavy weekend of entertainment and had not finished reading more than half the correspondence laid out for him.

"It's Mr Lawrence, sir."

"What does she want *now*, for heaven's sake?"

"No. Not *Mrs* Lawrence. Her husband, Mr Stone. I mean *Mr* Lawrence, sir."

"Are you mad? He's dead and buried."

"No." The young man was indignant. If Stone was too thick this morning to understand simple English he wasn't going to butter him up with any 'sirs' either. "The gentleman gives his name as Lawrence, James Lawrence, and wants to discuss, that's how he put it, The Old Farmhouse."

"Show him in to me, then," said Mr Stone, with whom the penny had dropped at last. "What are you waiting for, boy?"

The assistant, angered afresh, but a little reassured by the use of 'boy' instead of the more frequent 'clot', darted away, returning in a few seconds to announce "Mr Lawrence, sir," and disappear again, closing the boss's door behind him.

Mr Stone had risen as the visitor entered. He now stepped round his table with outstretched hand.

"Mr James Lawrence, I presume," he said, retrieving the hand from an uncomfortably firm grasp.

"That's right."

The newcomer pulled a chair close to the table and sat down. He had an envelope in his hands now, and pulling a letter from it passed this across the table to the estate agent.

"Save time if you read it first," he said. "Then we can talk about it properly."

Mr Stone could do no other than obey these brief definite instructions. The letter was a kind of introduction. It was addressed 'To all whom it may concern.' It notified all such that the bearer was a Mr James Lawrence, only son of Mr Jaspar Lawrence, late of The Old Farmhouse, Meadowfield, and of Hillside Farm, near Penrith, Cumbria. It explained that the said Mr Lawrence had permission to begin making arrangements for the disposal of these properties since he was the sole heir to them under the will of the late Mr Jaspar Lawrence, the said will now going through the process of obtaining probate. The undersigned were acting as executors and were in a proper legal position to endorse any proposed arrangements Mr Lawrence would make. The letter was signed for and on behalf of Messrs Boll, Shin and Gregg, solicitors, a firm in Carlisle.

Mr Stone nodded several times as he refolded the letter and returned it to its envelope. In doing so he noticed the address, seeing to his surprise that it had been sent to Ontario. He could not help exclaiming, "I thought you were in Spain?"

"Why Spain?"

The stranger seemed to be equally astonished.

"Only something Mrs Lawrence said. I understood — business — "

"I have a business in Canada. Not Spain."

Mr Stone apologised.

"I should like you to arrange to put The Old Farmhouse on the market. If you need any further authority than that letter, I should like you to confirm it by getting into touch with these people. I have, of course."

"Thank you." Mr Stone took the letter out of the envelope again to write down the solicitors' address and telephone number.

"And we must have a survey of the house and grounds: perhaps you could set about arranging for it. I will give you a cheque for a deposit if you will name a suitable sum."

This looked like business to Mr Stone. His manner began to brighten.

"I take it you will leave me an address where I can contact you," he said, seizing a large sheet of office paper and snapping open one of the three biros he carried in his breast pocket.

"The Sitting Duck Hotel here," Mr Lawrence told him. "I arrived yesterday afternoon. I shall be staying about a week. I want to see everyone who knew my father, both before he left Meadowfield and after he came back as an invalid."

Mr Stone followed his interesting visitor to the door. He had not been able to add anything to their conversation since Mr Lawrence had spoken of his father in a way that stifled comment or question. Moreover, he had said nothing about his wife, not a word. She might never have existed. Thinking over the gossip in the pub, which had been relayed to him — or had it — ?

Mr Stone, knowing he was not likely to remember which or how, felt a slight chill, a slight tremor in mid-abdomen. On his way back to his own room he paused beside his assistant's desk at the back of the outer office.

"When was the last time Mrs Lawrence came in about putting a board up on The Old Farmhouse?"

"Ten days, I think, sir."

"Last Friday week, right?"

"She said something about joining her husband soon."

"In Spain?"

"She didn't say so to me. But I asked for an address where we could reach her. She gave me — " He paused to flip through a file on his desk, but Mr Stone stopped him, picking up the file as he did so.

"I'll find it," he said. "You might look out and bring into my room every other file we possess on the Lawrence property. I have a feeling the Mr Lawrence who was in here just now is going to want to see the lot before he's done with us. Which is much more than his wife wanted when she thought I could sell the place for her over the counter."

"She doesn't seem to have joined him, does she?" the assistant said, eagerly. "I mean nobody's seen much of her since she came back from Seacombe. But she's here, so why is he staying at a hotel, I wonder?"

"And you know he is? You been snooping?"

"No, sir." The assistant was indignant. "He said he was going back to The Sitting Duck as he reached the door."

Mr Stone was pretty sure this was a lie, but it did not greatly matter. Lawrence would be in Meadowfield all the week: he would be going over the house with him on Wednesday. In the meantime he would write to the Carlisle solicitors to acknowledge their letter and describe his interview with the heir to the property. All without mentioning the latter's wife. To Mrs Lawrence he wrote with a similar description of the interview and the information that The Old Farmhouse would shortly be on the market. He addressed this letter to her at The Old Farmhouse, then sat looking at it, for it occurred to him that if the couple were both in Meadowfield surely Mr Lawrence would tell his wife what he was doing, even if he had put up at an hotel instead of going to the house. But if she had left again, as seemed likely, he ought to send it to Carlisle too. So he put it away in his drawer for unfinished business and turned the key on it. Then, reluctantly, he addressed himself to the next business of the day.

During that morning Mr Lawrence visited the church, where he found two parishioners watering and renovating the flowers in the chancel. From them he learned where he could expect to find the vicar or his wife and, to their disappointment, left them without explaining who he was or what he wanted.

To Mrs Gilman, who said the vicar was expected home shortly, he did explain who he was and suggested coming back in the afternoon. But the vicar arrived before his wife had found her diary of engagements.

The vicar shook Mr Lawrence warmly by the hand, saying to his wife, "Coffee, dear?" which sent her hurrying away.

"Sit down, Mr Lawrence," the vicar said. "I am very pleased to see you. We all are. Your family — "

"That's what I want to ask you about particularly," the visitor interrupted and went on in a rush of words, "I have blamed myself over and over for never coming back all these years!"

"*Years!*" the vicar was amazed. Mrs Gilman, bringing in a tray, nearly dropped it, hearing these words.

"Yes, years, I'm afraid," Mr Lawrence hurried on. "Forgive me, but you must be far too young to have known my father while he lived here with his mother. He left almost directly after he married my mother. I was born in the Lakes and brought up entirely in the north. He farmed for a time, but after my grandmother died he gave it up and went into business. So I followed the same line, agricultural supplies, only I thought I'd do better abroad. So I emigrated to Canada and I've been there ever since. I mean ever since I was twenty-five."

Mr Gilman wanted to ask so many questions that he could not decide how to begin. In the silence that followed Mrs Gilman said, "Let me fill your cup again, Mr Lawrence," and while she did so went on, "You know you are one of our most famous families at this end of Meadowfield. The memorials in the church — "

"Yes," Mr Lawrence said eagerly. "I do very much want to see them. My father used to say he ought to add my mother to the latest one. She died when I was twenty-four, but she was buried in the north. Her family were all there, that was why she didn't want to live down here."

"But she was married in Meadowfield," Mrs Gilman said, puzzled.

"Oh yes, her parents were here for a few years. That was how she met my father."

Mr Gilman looked at his watch, got up and put his cup on the tray.

"I don't want to hurry you," he said. "But I would very much like you to see the registers relating to your family. If we could go over to the church at once I could get them out for you."

Mr Lawrence was happy to agree. On the way there Mr Gilman talked about old Mr Lawrence; how he himself had gone to The Old Farmhouse to see if the invalid needed or wanted his services; how Mrs Lawrence had been helpful but there was little he could do with someone so afflicted; how the medical profession had been most interested, especially the physiotherapist, a splendid girl, also the young G.P.

"Yes," said Mr Lawrence," I particularly want to see anyone who was good to my father."

"Then I will tell them to get in contact. They are very busy people, as you must realise."

"I do that."

Still no word about Mrs Lawrence, or her part in looking after the old man; no word about his tragic death, or was it really so tragic for one in his terrible state of disablement and misery? Mr Gilman's curiosity, added to a real concern that justice must be done to all who served the afflicted, drove him to hint at his anxiety in this direction.

"I think Mrs Lawrence behaved wonderfully in looking after him," he said. "Only being a sort of relation, I mean."

"Yes, she did," Mr Lawrence answered and left it at that.

"While you were away — in Spain," the vicar said boldly.

"Canada. Not Spain."

"Never Spain? I understood — business — " Mr Gilman spread his hands.

"Oh, you mean the European market? Well, no, too complicated. Franco's death and all. We're not a very big firm."

"I see." The vicar did not see at all, but recovering his nerve he promised to get in touch with Lucy Summers and Geoff Harris and send them along to The Sitting Duck if possible some time that evening, or the next.

The vicar's note reached Lucy on her return to her flat at the end of the day's work. It was handed to her by Sue, who had spoken to Mrs Gilman earlier the same afternoon when the latter had brought the note.

"Mr Lawrence," Sue chattered, before Lucy had had time to open the envelope. "*The* Mr Lawrence. And he's been in Canada all this time and — "

"Oh, shut up, can't you!" Lucy said crossly, trying to decide whether or not to change before meeting this somewhat mysterious character. Wisely she decided to go as she was. A man who had not tried to see his father after that severe stroke, had not attended the inquest or funeral in Seacombe, nor even after this length of time done anything at all for his wife, did not rate any kind of consideration, any oblique respect for the dead, for family feeling. He had shown none.

So Lucy simply put a comb through her hair, straightened her neat trouser suit and went back to her little car which she had not yet put in the garage. She drove rapidly to The Sitting Duck where she met Geoff Harris pushing his way in through revolving doors.

"Hallo!" he said. "Word from the vicar, too?"

"That's right."

"Surprise, surprise. Lawrence himself at last, it seems."

"He's left it pretty late."

"You can say that again."

James Lawrence was expecting them. He had a tray of drinks already waiting in his room, which Geoff considered showed the right spirit and Lucy thought was on a par with his proved callousness. However, they both accepted glasses and sat down, waiting for their host to begin the interview.

This he did in much the same manner he had used with the vicar. He began with a few words about his father and about his own life in the North of England and then explained why he had come over from Canada.

"Apart from dealing with my father's properties here I do particularly want to see anyone who knew him and helped him in the last weeks of his life. Mr Gilman was very helpful. It was he who put me on to you two. I suppose I can see the hospital reports and all that sort of thing, Dr Harris?"

"I'm sure the Hospital Secretary will let you see anything you ask him for. They call them Administrative Officers now, not Secretaries," Guy told him.

"But you were his family doctor, weren't you?"

"G.P. yes. For the few weeks he was here, after the hospital at Lincoln discharged him fit to travel. Our hospital here did put him up for a few days while Mrs Lawrence got The Old Farmhouse ready for him. Then we took over; my firm, I mean. There are four of us, in partnership."

Mr Lawrence frowned.

"I was told he'd been in Lincoln," he said, slowly. "I can't understand why."

Lucy exclaimed, but Geoff stopped her, pulling a folded letter out of his pocket.

"I — we — Miss Summers and I went to Lincoln. Your father's address there was on the Lincoln Hospital report.

We saw the house where he'd stayed the two nights before his stroke. He'd booked the rooms in advance. I got this from the landlady, Mrs Smith. Read it."

Lucy could not keep silent any longer.

"He knows his father was there, Geoff. You were there, Mr Lawrence, Mrs Smith told us so. Didn't she, Geoff?"

"Of course she did. What about it, sir?"

Four young accusing eyes stared at Mr Lawrence. He stared back at them, then took his father's letter from Geoff, unfolded and read it. When he looked up his face had set into hard lines but his eyes shone bright.

"I came over from Canada two days ago," he said. "The first time for over twelve years. Whoever was there in Lincoln with my father was not me."

He drew a long breath.

"Now tell me about Dad. You first, doctor."

Geoff described what he had seen of the patient, what he had ordered in the way of treatment, and that he had advised a return to hospital, but this never took place, because Mrs Lawrence had taken him away to the seaside.

"Miss Summers?" Mr Lawrence asked.

She did not speak at once. The shock of knowing how Mrs Lawrence must have betrayed this man with whoever had joined her in Lincoln — With her husband away, so far away, Canada, not Spain. She had never really trusted Mrs Lawrence. Now she was ready to believe anything of the woman; anything at all.

"Miss Summers?" said Mr Lawrence again.

"I think — I thought the first time I saw him, I told Geoff here, that he was starving, really, literally, starving for food. We couldn't prove — we tried — that's why we went to Lincoln — I'm sorry — I'm — "

Lucy was crying, all her passionate concern for the helpless old man, so long suppressed, so hopelessly frustrated by the non-believers, the liars, the twisters, of whom that elegant, quiet, cold-eyed woman was the chief, now broke from her in desperate, child-like, sobs and tears.

"What is she trying to tell me, Dr Harris?" Mr Lawrence's stern voice demanded, while at the same time he reached for Lucy's glass, refilled it and pushed it across to her.

Geoff did so, in full detail, not forgetting the consultant psychiatrist's opinion and the attempts of the Social Services. During his explanation Lucy recovered herself enough to apologise for her unseemly breakdown.

"My dear," said Mr Lawrence, quite gently, "it did you credit."

"But why?" Lucy asked him, encouraged by this remark. "Why did you never come to help your wife, why send her to look after your father alone? We all thought that man at Lincoln was you. He never came here, you see."

Mr Lawrence beat a hand on the arm of his chair.

"My wife," he said, "is in Canada with my children and has always been there."

"Then she isn't Mrs Lawrence! This woman who — "

"She is Mrs Lawrence all right," he told his startled visitors. "She is Jaspar Lawrence's second wife. She is my stepmother!"

His bitter laugh struck the air like a whip.

10

Soon after the young people, still very much sobered, even shocked, by their discovery of Mrs Lawrence's true relationship with their patient, had left The Sitting Duck, reception rang up Mr Lawrence to announce another visitor.

"Who is it?" he asked.

He heard a brief discussion. Then a new voice said, "The name's Tine. I represent — "

"O.K. Come up."

Obviously this was the press, he decided. And reasonably polite, too. Mustn't antagonise anyone if he wanted to avoid any more muddles and deceptions.

Mr Lawrence rinsed the used glasses under the tap in his bathroom and returned them to the tray in time to answer the newcomer's knock.

"I suppose you're the press," he said. "I don't mind putting you in the picture about my arrival here, but I'd like to know why you think it important enough to want an interview. What'll you have?"

The young man, somewhat overwhelmed by this beginning, asked for a beer and then said awkwardly, but truthfully, "Well, sir, on account of the rumours going about today regarding the disappearance of Mrs Lawrence. You see, sir, your wife — "

"My wife," said Mr Lawrence, repeating his statement to Geoff and Lucy, "is in Canada. The lady you refer to, who has been staying at The Old Farmhouse recently, is my father's widow."

"Your *father*'s — !"

Mr Lawrence found the reporter's blank astonishment annoying.

"Widow," he repeated. "My father, Jaspar Lawrence's second wife, whom he married five years ago. I have not met the lady. I live in Canada. I heard of my father's death from his solicitors, who are in Carlisle. I was informed of his illness at the same time. Not before."

Tine, who had begun to scribble at speed, looked up as Mr Lawrence stopped speaking.

"Not before?" he repeated. "Pardon me, but do I infer you had no previous knowledge of old Mr Lawrence's, I mean your father's, stroke?"

"That was what I meant. No. I was not told."

"But Mrs Lawrence did write after the accident, the fatal accident at Seacombe? To explain the full circumstances?"

"No, young man, she did not write. But my father's lawyer wrote."

He paused; his face was serious, apart from his eyes that showed clearly his amusement at the journalist's perplexity. "I am here in England to wind up my father's affairs, which in Meadowfield means The Old Farmhouse. I shall be going over the place tomorrow with the agent. After that I go north to deal with his other property, Hillside Farm near Penrith."

He paused again, but seeing Tine's intention to begin another spate of questions, he got up saying, "I suggest you drink up and carry what I have told you to your editor. You can add that I have no intention of discussing family matters in public."

"But Mrs Lawrence — "

"My father's widow is not my responsibility. I have no idea where she is or when she left Meadowfield. Probably she has gone to Hillside in order to see the lawyers."

"But people are saying — "

"If you believe gossip you may risk libel," Mr Lawrence said firmly. "So you'd better be careful. Off you go, now."

At which blunt direction Tine, hearing authority unveiled, choked on the last mouthful of his beer, but recovered enough to express his thanks before the closing door pushed him gently into the corridor.

"Unco-operative, eh?" said the editor sourly.

"I'll say."

"Bullying? Threatened a libel action?"

"Well, no. Not exactly."

"How'd you mean, then?"

"Refused to say anything on family matters was how he put it. That was after he broke it Mrs Lawrence was not his wife, but his stepmother. Naturally I wanted to follow up that angle. He must be just about her age, you see. Not much younger. Say's he's never met her, being in Canada. She never wrote to him about the old man's stroke, he says."

"Um." The editor was thoughtful, humming softly. "I wonder if she knew his address? Looks like some kind of family feud, wouldn't you say? Get hold of the northern locals, Tine. See if you can find any reference to the family in the notices of the accident."

"There was nothing in the *Seacombe Star*," Tine offered. "I looked before I went to The Sitting Duck."

"Good boy. Try Seacombe again, then. And after that Carlisle. And then you might sort out the gossip about Sunday evening. Who saw what and when. At the Farmhouse windows or in the garden or in the road."

"He'll be seeing over the house tomorrow, he said," Tine offered eagerly. "Shall I — ?"

"No," said his editor. "You've got enough on your plate, with what I've just given you. Don't be greedy, mate."

What he really meant was he would send someone a lot more forceful to cope with the combination of owner and agent. Tine guessed this, swallowing his partial failure and his pride. Already he was thinking up ways of putting off, even to the point of bribery, any competitor in news-gathering. He was thankful he was still to work on the story. The woman, now, who had seen Mrs Lawrence at the window, looking at the rain and waving. 'Not waving, but drowning'. The famous line, a cliché, of course, but might it be true? Not literally, but an empty house — The visitor — The garden prowler — The anorak —

Young Tine settled down to tackle the northern locals and the *Seacombe Star*.

After a good lunch at The Sitting Duck, undisturbed by fresh visitors, Mr Lawrence decided to visit Mrs Chandler at her office. It was only fair, he thought, to hear her account of the efforts the Social Services had made to help his father.

There was the usual protocol: the usual attempt to promote a non-existent authority.

"Have you an appointment with Mrs Chandler?" Beryl, her secretary, asked him.

"Of course not," Mr Lawrence said briskly. "I told you. I got here only the day before yesterday. Sunday, if you remember."

The girl, flushing at the hint of criticism, said she would enquire. After about twenty minutes he was admitted to Mrs Chandler's room. Judging by the open file on her desk he decided that she had already briefed herself on his case. Perhaps she was not so dim as the young medicals had led him to expect.

He approached with hand outstretched. Mrs Chandler, surprised by this unexpected action, stumbled to her feet, knocked the file to the floor, dived to retrieve it, missed, found herself steadied by the outstretched hand and returned to her chair with her papers restored.

"Thank you," she panted. "Clumsy of me." Anger replaced relief. "I did not expect — "

"To see me today. No," said Mr Lawrence. "May I sit down?"

"Of course."

He drew a chair up to the desk and sat, pointing a finger at the file, whose ruffled pages Mrs Chandler was smoothing nervously.

"I take it that refers to my father? I have come to Meadowfield to settle his affairs and to you to say thank you for your various efforts on his behalf. I take it you were working in conjunction with the doctors. I'm sure my father was grateful, even if he could never speak his thanks."

Mrs Chandler recovered a little. These were words she always liked and expected to hear, even though the present speaker was so totally unlike the man Dorothy Lawrence had led her to expect. But his prolonged, his unexplained, absence. That was still most confusing. It matched neither this visitor's appearance nor his words.

She said, carefully, "Our Miss Carr, she is a psychiatric social worker, did visit him on the recommendation of the psychiatrist, Dr Fairclough. That was for speech therapy."

"Did Miss Carr give him speech therapy? I understood from his G.P., Dr Harris, that she had no training in it? Is that so?"

"Well, actually no, she is not really a speech therapist. But we had no one available for that. I sent her along more to assess the position psychologically."

"I should have thought this Dr Fairclough's opinion had already established that. A consultant, after all."

"We like to make our own assessments where it is a question of allocating scarce personnel."

"I see," said Mr Lawrence, whose stern face and critical eyes disturbed Mrs Chandler so much that she cried impulsively, "After all, Mr Lawrence, you took no steps yourself, did you, to see your father or to arrange for his care and treatment? You thought more of your business in Spain. You left it all to your wife — "

"Stop!" cried Mr Lawrence, in a sudden consuming

99

rage. This was really the outside bloody limit! "You at least should have found out who this Mrs Lawrence really was. No, don't interrupt! Listen to me, you self-important, inefficient, ignorant woman! If you ring that bell I'll — Now, sit still and listen to a few *facts* for a change!"

As his fury subsided he gave her all that he had explained to Mr Stone and Mr Gilman and a bit more detail he had learned from the family solicitors and bankers in Carlisle and Meadowfield.

"Did you ever make the slightest effort to discover her real financial position?" he asked, when he had done with explanations.

Mrs Chandler, white-faced and subdued, answered in a low voice, "She had a bank card."

"Of course. But the branch here are in touch with the Carlisle branch and both were in touch with my father's lawyers. Were you in touch with them, ever?"

"I saw no necessity."

"And no need to get into direct touch with the man she said was her husband?"

"She never said that. Well, only by inference. That he was her husband. She always spoke of him as Jim. Short for James, of course. I took that for granted."

"What did she call my father? Poor old boy, he couldn't contradict her."

"She called him Mr Lawrence in speaking of him. In fact," Mrs Chandler said, recovering enough to show resentment, "Mrs Lawrence never once, in my presence, claimed to be other than she was. Mrs Lawrence."

"Naturally. She is Mrs Lawrence. But you believed her? You trusted her?"

"I saw no reason to disbelieve her." Rallying still further Mrs Chandler said, "I am not in the habit of suspecting my clients of deliberate deceit. I can see you take a different view, Mr Lawrence. No doubt prompted by your natural jealousy at your father's re-marriage to a much younger woman. That is most understandable."

100

"It isn't! It's bloody bosh!" said Mr Lawrence, rudely, springing to his feet.

There was no handshake as they said a very cold goodbye to one another at the door of Mrs Chandler's room.

She went back to her desk feeling more upset by this interview than by any of the more or less puzzling cases that had come her way in the last few months.

Not that her opinion of Dorothy Lawrence had altered in any respect, except to wonder what sort of pressure had led her, such an attractive, still young woman, to marry that horrid old man, more than thirty years older than herself. Perhaps he had not been so dreadful as she herself imagined him. Not before his stroke. She had always rather shrunk from visiting those cases when she was on field work in her own young days. And this son of his, however, boorish, ill-mannered, coarse, was undoubtedly good-looking, and he wasn't in his first youth either.

She picked up the outside phone and tried to get Hillside Farm. That was the number Mrs Lawrence had given her when she had explained that she expected to meet Jim soon, on his return from Spain.

Mrs Chandler winced as she recollected this conversation. Jim. Not James Lawrence. Not Spain. Why not? Who was Jim? Poor poor Dorothy Lawrence!

The bell was ringing at Hillside Farm. No one answered it. After two minutes Mrs Chandler rang off. Dorothy wouldn't be there. Then where was she?

For the first time since the weekend Mrs Chandler went over in her mind the various scraps of gossip that were spreading and growing in the town. She even began to write them down on a sheet of clean paper. She rang up Nurse Parfit, who had spoken already to most of the neighbours in Lawn Road. She rang up Elaine Brigg in Seacombe to discover if Mr Lawrence's son had been in touch with her. Elaine, she found, was better informed than herself. After the accident, at the inquest, her client's real relationship with the deceased had been stated by a solicitor. Mrs Lawrence had been too ill from shock to appear in court. The occurrence had not been regarded with undue excitement in the tourist town, happening as it did, to a stranger. In the big dailies the question of safety on the pier, where ferries arrived, had been given prior importance.

It had been in Meadowfield that the accident had caused more interest. This had been centred on the fate of the old invalid, Mrs Chandler remembered, rather than on Mrs Lawrence. It had always been assumed in Meadowfield that she was his daughter-in-law. The truth had been passed over. She had come back to The Old Farmhouse; she had been unhappy, in difficulties; now she had vanished. No one had seen her leave the house on that wet Sunday night.

Mrs Chandler put away her list of gossip items with an inward shudder. Where was poor Dorothy Lawrence now?

On Wednesday morning Mr Lawrence, Mr Stone and an assistant surveyor went through the garden gate of The Old Farmhouse and began to inspect the property from the outside. Mr Stone had already satisfied himself that the house was empty, though he had done no more on Tuesday evening than ring the bell several times and look in through the mainly uncurtained windows. He had noted that the ancient shutters at the kitchen windows were closed, but this had not aroused his curiosity sufficiently to suggest a solo entry, though he had the keys in his pocket, where they still lay. He was pleased to see that all the outside drains were unblocked, not filled with dead leaves or other rubbish. He saw that the cellar window had a piece of metal propped against it and he left that as it was.

The tour of the garden, therefore, was leisurely. Its neglect was very obvious, but as Mr Stone pointed out, Mr and Mrs Lawrence had been in residence only a little over three months, including their absence in Seacombe and before that the house had lain empty for two years.

"Not that the last tenants did much about the garden," Mr Stone explained. "A shame, really. My late partner always said it was a picture in old Mrs Lawrence's day. But of course she had a regular gardener then."

"I know," Mr Lawrence answered. "Don't forget my father lived here too and kept up the farm for the last ten years or so before he married. He always said the flower garden was a joy and his mother looked after it herself. The gardener did the vegetables."

"The house was always let furnished," Mr Stone added, "to get over any trouble about ending the tenancies. That was before any letting at all really means handing over the property, furniture and all."

"Crazy," agreed Mr Lawrence. "You must sell now, not let."

"Of course," Mr Stone agreed.

They were standing looking into the jungle of weeds, enclosed by walls, that had been the vegetable garden. Withered branches of fruit trees hung from rusty wires, long trailing nettles lay across the paths. They turned away in silence. James Lawrence had never known his grandmother, but he understood a little of what his poor afflicted father must have felt when he saw this devastation from his wheeled chair. If his young wife ever allowed him to see it.

Mr Stone thought it was time to leave the garden and learn the worst about the inside of the house. It should not be too bad, he decided, trying to remember how long it was since he had taken round prospective tenants. A bit gloomy, needing a lick of paint here and there. Old Mr Lawrence's letter announcing his return had not asked for redecoration. Perhaps he had meant to put it in hand when he arrived. Only that had been postponed for a month after his stroke and Mrs Lawrence had never asked for any improvements later.

Leaving the surveyor to get on with the general measurements in the garden Mr Stone led the way to the front door, unlocked it and stood aside for Mr Lawrence to go in.

They walked into three rooms that led off the wide hall. Mr Lawrence noted a good deal of old-fashioned, undistinguished Victorian pieces of furniture and one or two attractive farmhouse dressers and tables of an earlier date. Dust everywhere and no polish. A pile of cigarette ends in a bowl in the long room that looked out at Lawn Road in front, through the gap in the tall hedge where the gate stood.

Mr Lawrence felt more and more depressed by what he saw. He cursed his stepmother for not being here to show him round and settle her business with him *now*, no more delays and uncertainties. So that he could get back to Canada, to his real life. Away from all this nostalgia, made so much more painful by the neglect and grime engulfing those second-hand memories of the past.

Mr Stone held an open sheet of stiff paper, bearing a plan of the inside of the house.

"The kitchen premises are this way," he said, moving off as he spoke. He pushed open a door at the end of the hall, and stepped inside. It was dark there; he found and switched on the light. Mr Lawrence, pausing to look at an old print on the wall of the passage, heard him exclaim aloud.

If the other ground floor rooms had been sadly empty, vague ghosts murmuring from yellow photographs, the kitchen was an all too recent battlefield, a scream of fury, a yell of violence. There were broken crockery and glass, spilt food, half a loaf in one corner a broken gin bottle in another.

"Breaking and entering," muttered Mr Stone, going towards the shuttered window.

"Better not touch anything," Mr Lawrence warned him and added, "If the phone's working we'd better get the police at once!"

104

But Mr Stone, though he left the windows untouched, was trying the back door and found it both locked and bolted on the inside. He went back to the littered table to spread out his plan.

"Whoever was in here to make this mess must have gone out by the front door. Someone did see a character prowling in the garden on Sunday night. Someone else says they saw someone in the road in the small hours. There's been a fight here or something like it."

"And you say the reports mention only *one* person?"

Mr Stone pointed to his plan.

"This door," he said, pointing to one next to the kitchen and just outside in the hall. "It's the cellar. Has a window on to the garden."

"And steps or a ladder down into it," added Mr Lawrence, stooping to the plan.

"Yes. I remember it. A ladder. There was a light on the wall just inside. I put it on the last time I went down. Over two years, the bulb may have gone. Be careful, Mr Lawrence!"

For the latter had moved and was shaking the door of the cellar. "Locked," he said.

"I've got a spare key. Here. Wait a minute. I'll put the hall light on."

He did so. Mr Lawrence opened the door, letting it swing forward as he reached inside for the light.

"Don't move!" shrieked Mr Stone at his side. "The ladder — *Gone!*"

They both shrank back from the void below them, peering down as the door began to swing shut again.

They clutched one another's arms; Mr Stone was white-faced, shaking.

"Did you see — Lying — ! Oh, my God!" He leaned on the opposite wall.

"A body on the floor below," said Mr Lawrence in a hard voice. "Now I really will get on to the coppers."

11

SERGEANT THOMAS WITH Constable Hill got the message in their patrol car about a quarter of a mile from Lawn Road. They reached The Old Farmhouse in less than five minutes, so soon that neither Stone nor James Lawrence had fully recovered from the impact of what they had seen.

"A body?" Sergeant Thomas asked. "Man or woman?"

"We didn't have time to see before the cellar door swung shut," Lawrence said. "Then I went to ring up and you arrived before I got back to Stone."

As the estate agent was sitting on a chair in the hall with his head in his hands, moaning faintly, the sergeant continued to speak to Mr Lawrence while the constable found his way to the kitchen. Here the signs of violence checked him for a second, but nevertheless he took a clean tumbler from an open cupboard, filled it with water from the tap and took it back to the hall, where Mr Stone received it gratefully.

"I want you over here," said Sergeant Thomas to Hill.

"Right, sarge," answered the constable, abandoning Mr Stone.

"Hold this door open and shine your torch down." They both peered cautiously into the abyss. "I'd say from here it was a man," he went on, appealing to Mr Lawrence, who was staring over his shoulder. "But that's only a guess."

"Probably," answered the latter. "A man."

"Not your — " The Meadowfield police had learned with amusement that the visiting male Lawrence, far from being Mrs Lawrence's husband was, unlikely as it seemed, her stepson.

"You were going to say wife?" Mr Lawrence smiled bitterly. He was sufficiently upset to forget his own ban on giving family history to strangers. "I couldn't possibly say whether that's my stepmother or the boy-friend she seems to have been calling Jim. No, I couldn't say in any case because I have never seen my father's widow. I was in Canada when he married her. It seems to have been a very quiet, Register Office affair. Dad wrote to me after it was done. Apologetic. Knew I wouldn't approve. Said she was much younger than himself."

Sergeant Thomas was on his knees, feeling the edge of the floorboards. He slid down further, until he was lying on his stomach with his arms reaching into the drop.

"I've got the two rings in the wall," he reported, looking up sideways. "Not broken off. They've got the hooks from the ladder stuck in them, with — yes, jagged edges of wood on the hooks, from the ladder itself. You have a go, Dick."

He took over the torch, while his junior lay down, squirming very cautiously into position and saying, "Want me to feel for the steps, sarge? You ought to have a dekko at the kitchen. Hooligans gone to town there!"

"I was just going to tell you about that," Mr Lawrence put in. "Stone and I went in just before we opened this cellar door. I was going to have rung you anyway."

"I'll take the torch if you like," Mr Stone said. "I'm all right now."

Ignorant of the drama inside the house, the assistant surveyor, after completing his measurements of the garden boundaries and lay-out, was circling the house to inspect the drains and other outlets. He had reached the cellar window, and to help him with his inspection now threw aside the piece of tin covering it. Inside therefore, the cellar was suddenly drenched in bright daylight, the cobwebbed, matted rubbish of past years lay revealed and also the blood-stained figure of a man, crumpled into an awkward heap. One twisted leg trailed behind him, one arm was thrown forward. The dark hair matted with dried blood that had dripped forward over the face hid the features apart from the staring eyes. But these were directed upward and the whole position of the corpse suggested that before the final collapse a desperate effort had been made, at least to move.

Constable Hill squirmed a little nearer to the edge and peered over. The steps, as he expected, were leaning against the wall of the cellar at a very awkward angle. They did not appear to be broken, but the jagged ends at the top matched those attached to the hooks that Sergeant Thomas had felt. Also separate from the steps, lying beside them, was a pair of handles that must have been screwed to the floor at the top of the steps on either side.

"Looks as if they'd been sawn off and unscrewed on purpose," Hill reported. "Then the whole ladder could be given a push or levered away somehow."

He scrambled back from the drop, got to his feet and began to brush himself down with his hands.

Sergeant Thomas, behind him, said curtly, "Go out and tell Mr Stone's assistant to come indoors. Then you can wait in the road for the doctor and the ambulance. Better move our car further up the road, first."

"We'll need another ladder," Mr Lawrence said, "before we can get down there."

"Yes, sir," answered Thomas. "I did think of that."

He was feeling justly aggrieved. Here was a complicated, a serious situation, a possible booby trap, with hideous results and he could not even take a preliminary look at the corpse. Unless —

He turned to Mr Stone.

"You wouldn't know if there was a garden ladder in the garage, sir, or a toolshed that might have one?"

"There's no car, but I've got the garage key here," Mr

Stone told him. "There's only a small toolshed." He turned to his assistant and together they moved towards the kitchen.

"Front door, please sir. We don't want more prints than we can help in the kitchen."

Mr Lawrence had watched Sergeant Thomas and understood his impatience, though not the real cause. So when he suggested mildly that they might as well have a look upstairs for Mrs Lawrence, he was met with suppressed fury.

"*Mrs Lawrence!* How do we know it isn't her in the cellar?"

"We don't. But it looks like a man, didn't we agree?"

"I'm not guessing."

But he was doing so before, Lawrence remembered. This was childish. He said coldly, "No objection to my having a quick look, is there? After all, the place belongs to me."

"If you insist I can't stop you," the sergeant said. "But I warn you I shall mention it in my report."

"Don't be difficult," Mr Lawrence told him, making for the stairs. "If I find another body, I'll give you a shout. But I promise not to touch anything."

He was gone and Sergeant Thomas remained in the hall, fuming. He was only slightly mollified by the return of the house agent and the surveyor, carrying between them a fairly long ladder. The front door was held open for them by a third figure whom Thomas recognised.

"No!" he shouted. "Go away, young Tine! We don't want the press here yet."

"We don't want the press here at all, ever," cried Mr Lawrence, running down the stairs again.

Tine stood just inside the door, grinning. He had been warned off The Old Farmhouse by his editor, but happening to see a police car outside —

"Mr Stone's given me the drama," he said. "You wouldn't want me to scoop just that. Not on top of all the gossip with no identification. You and the Super wouldn't like that, Mr Thomas, I'm sure."

Sergeant Thomas took a step towards the young man, his right hand clenched in anger, but not yet raised. However, his mood and behaviour changed instantly as Hill pushed Tine out of his way to announce the arrival of the ambulance, followed by another police car.

"Detective Chief Inspector Bartlet, sarge," he announced, opening the front door wider as a tall figure in a dark grey suit walked past him into the hall.

Mr Lawrence stepped forward at the same moment as Sergeant Thomas and both men began to speak. The newcomer held up a hand and then dealt with the strained situation in masterly fashion.

"You will be Mr James Lawrence, sir, I take it," he said, speaking rapidly and clearly. "And you and Mr Stone found this body in the cellar when you were inspecting the house together. Yes, Sergeant Thomas," he went on, turning to the scarlet-faced policeman, "fix the ladder with Hill, will you? Then we can get on with the job."

"Sir," said Thomas, taking the surveyor's place at the near end of the ladder, while Hill relieved Mr Stone at the back end.

While the Law was arranging access to the cellar the Detective Chief Inspector listened to the full story of the find.

"Cellar door locked, but no key?" he asked.

"None this side."

"Light not on?"

"No. The drop would be invisible without it," Stone said. "The light switch is just inside the door: you could reach it at once when the door opened — outwards — without taking more than one step forward. The ladder top, which has upright handles, would be visible at once."

"When the light went on?"

"Exactly."

"Or in daylight?"

110

"Yes. If the cellar window was not obscured."

This led to a further explanation of the surveyor's action in the garden, at the end of which Mr Lawrence, whose impatience was growing stronger every second said roughly, "Booby trap. Obvious. But who for and who by?"

Any answer Detective Chief Inspector Bartlet thought of giving was prevented by action from two directions. Thomas and Hill came back to say that the ladder was in position and Dr Geoffrey Harris walked in through the open front door. He greeted Mr Lawrence, nodded to Mr Stone and addressed the Chief Inspector by name, adding, "Dr McMann asked me to come over at once, because he's bogged down with an emergency and my other partners are still seeing patients at the clinic. I hope you don't mind."

"I'll put up with it this time, doctor," Bartlet told him. He knew Geoff Harris by sight and by a growing reputation for quick action and careful work. Youth and inexperience need not count in the preliminaries of this case, he thought, though it remained to be proved.

"This way, sir," he said, adding as they reached the open cellar door, "Sergeant Thomas will show you. I'll follow you down."

"Can I come too?" asked Mr Lawrence.

"Later," answered Bartlet. But he turned to Hill and said, "Photographs. And then hold the ambulance people. We don't want a bigger crowd than we have already."

This seemed to Mr Stone to be a hint. Mr Lawrence understood it as such, but was determined to stay.

"I'll get in touch later today," he said. "I'm sure you want to be off."

As Bartlet paid no attention to either of them, the estate agent and his surveyor went away, escaping from Tine by leaving through the garage and stooping under cover of the police cars until they reached their own.

Meanwhile Geoff conducted a brief examination of the distorted body of the dead man. For a man it proved to be

111

in spite of the large mop of dark hair that concealed recently clipped sideburns and a three or four days' beard.

He must have stepped off the fifteen feet drop while moving forward into the dark cellar. One femur was broken midway between hip and knee. The other leg had a cracked ankle, the left arm a broken wrist. In collapsing forward on impact he had struck his head, or so Geoff supposed, against a glass mirror, a piece of furniture discarded for years that seemed to have been propped up on a worn-out old casual table. The mirror's frame was broken, the shattered glass was bloodstained.

"Cuts all about his head and neck," Geoff reported. "Some quite deep. Must have lost a lot of blood."

"But did not kill himself right away?" suggested Bartlet.

"No. Not for some time. As you see, he made an attempt to crawl towards where he imagined the ladder ought to be."

"How could he imagine that, if the cellar light was not on and no light — even on that stormy night there were street lamps — could get in past the metal plate outside, propped against the window."

Geoff thought, then said with inward horror, "If there was a light on in the hall and it showed under the foot of the door?"

"That's exactly what was in my mind," said the Detective Chief Inspector.

The police photographer took pictures of the body from above and below, and a close-up from either side. He also photographed the broken mirror and the cellar ladder where it leaned precariously against the wall with its detached handles beside it.

When he had finished his work he climbed up again, followed slowly by the other two.

"Can I go down now?" Mr Lawrence asked as they re-appeared in the hall.

"If you must," said Bartlet and to Thomas, "Take Mr Lawrence down, Sergeant, but don't let him touch anything." Before he continued on his way to the front door he added, "Because we shall be taking an extensive number of fingerprints, you see."

"Yes," said Mr Lawrence.

So they suspected foul play. Well, they could hardly avoid it. He had suspected it all along. And they still hadn't searched the house for the widow, had they?

He climbed down the ladder after Sergeant Thomas. It was not a pretty sight there on the cellar floor. He imagined the poor devil, shouting for help, weakening slowly as shock and loss of blood and the pain of his desperate efforts drove him deeper into death. If it hadn't been for the storm — If it hadn't been for the covered window — If it hadn't been for the rain —

The police had The Old Farmhouse to themselves for the rest of that day. They went over it very carefully indeed. They found a great deal of particular interest, but they did not find Mrs Lawrence.

On the other hand at the police station Mr Lawrence gave them a straightforward but limited account of his father's second marriage, not in any way concealing his poor opinion of it.

"He seems to have met her about five years ago in Lincoln," he explained. "She was working for some agricultural suppliers who were promoting an irrigation scheme for the Wash. My father had an idea for Morcombe Bay. He wrote several letters to me about it."

"Mentioning Mrs Lawrence by name? Her maiden name?"

"Not a word, the old rogue. Not until after he'd married her."

"Did she stay with the Lincoln firm until she left to get married? No, you won't know, but we can find out in Lincoln."

Bartlet looked at the stepson of the missing woman. A strong face, a strong straightforward character, he guessed.

He would never conceal his dislike of people, but he had far too much commonsense and normal good principles ever to attack them physically. He would be ruthless, though, in revengé for an injury. He hated Mrs Lawrence all right; he probably felt disappointed that her body had not been found, as well as that of the poor wretch in the cellar. But he doubted that they would find her anywhere in Meadowfield, though now they might be able to trace both her origins and her present whereabouts.

"Well, thank you for your help, sir," he said. "You won't be leaving Meadowfield just yet, will you? After the inquest, perhaps. But not back to Canada immediately, even then."

"You needn't worry," Mr Lawrence told him. "I want to get to the bottom of this just as much as you do."

He left the police station feeling pleased that Bartlet had not asked him anything about his own movements on the evening of his arrival. After all, why should he? No doubt The Sitting Duck had said he had arrived, gone out, been overtaken by the storm, had sheltered somewhere and come back after the rain had eased a bit. Right. Let them go on thinking that. At present anyhow. It was true, too. If they did ask for more he would give it to them.

He waited impatiently for the inquest, but was disappointed. The accident was described and the cause of death briefly stated. But as yet there had been no identification. Nothing on the body to help. Some photographs had been produced to the coroner, but not given to the press. The inquest was adjourned for three weeks.

Mr Lawrence left the court and went back to his hotel to ring up Geoff Harris. He had to ring up the surgery several times before he managed to persuade the guardian secretaries there to put him through.

"Bogged down," he commented, when they had exchanged regrets at the lack of progress, "on account of no identification. But I think I'm right in remembering you told me you had been to Lincoln."

"That's right," Geoff sounded excited. "Lucy and I went to try to check on Mr Lawrence's lodgings and I thought I might get a bit more than the bare report if I actually spoke to the chaps at the hospital who'd treated the old boy — sorry, your father — from the start."

"Exactly. Well, I should like to take you and the girl up there again to see the landlady and perhaps identify the villain who pretended to be my father's son. Any chance of you coming? Both of you? I'll lay on transport."

Geoff thought rapidly, calculating his next full day off duty. He gave the date.

"O.K. by me," Lawrence agreed. "And the girl?"

"I'll try to fix that, too."

"And if possible one of those photos the coroner was passed so cagily. I knew they wouldn't give me one, so I didn't ask."

"I'll see what I can do."

Mr Lawrence felt pleased with himself. He next rang up the agricultural supplier's firm in Lincoln where the second Mrs Lawrence had worked. He made an appointment to see their managing director on the day he was to be there. He stressed his position in Canada as a farmer in the grain area of that great country.

Then, feeling still more pleased with himself, he went down to lunch in the hotel's buffet bar.

12

UNTIL THEY REACHED the outskirts of Lincoln Geoff and Lucy had very little idea of the object of their presence in Mr Lawrence's car, beyond the proposed confrontation of the guest house manageress, Mrs Smith, with the true James Lawrence.

Geoff was driving the hired Rover.

"You know the route," Mr Lawrence told him, "and you normally drive on the left here. I don't. It doesn't bother me in the town but it does when I get out in the open and don't concentrate so hard. Lucy can go in front with you. I've got some work to do." He patted the briefcase he was carrying. "I'll get on with it in the back. Just pull up when we get near Lincoln, so I can give you my idea of how we ought to manage this meeting without scaring the pants off the old biddy who runs the lodging house."

So the drive went forward, very swiftly and smoothly, in far less time than on the first occasion, and to everyone's satisfaction. Geoff pulled up in a lay-by when the cathedral was in sight at the top of its hill. Lucy leaned back, admiring the view, while Geoff turned round to draw Mr Lawrence's attention to it.

"Nearly there, are we?" the latter said, quite unimpressed.

"The cathedral — " Lucy murmured.

"Now I think," Mr Lawrence went on, disregarding

her, "it will be best if you take me first to the offices of this firm."

He showed Geoff a letter from the agricultural suppliers. There was a small map beside the letter heading, showing the position of the building. "I imagine they have warehouses and so on somewhere else. The point is my father met his second wife when he visited the firm in the way of business. I want to find out what they know of her. But I'd like you two to leave me there and go to the lodgings and chat up the owner, find out if she knew Dorothy before she married my father. Find out if she'd ever met the man who pretended to be me."

"I don't think so," Geoff said. "None of them, really — "

"Then how the hell did she think Dad knew of her boarding house?"

"Guest house," said Lucy, beginning to resent his manner.

"Beg its pardon, guest house. It isn't like my father to go to a place like that instead of an hotel. He didn't want luxury, just reasonable comfort."

"You mean," Geoff said, to change the direction of the argument, "if Mrs Lawrence worked in Lincoln she may have been living at the guest house until she left to be married."

"Something of the sort," Mr Lawrence agreed.

The plan worked smoothly. The guest house door was opened by a young girl in an overall, who let them in without question, but left them in the hall until Mrs Smith appeared, which she did almost at once.

"Oh, it's you two," she said. "I thought it might be. Well, what can I do for you now?"

"It's about Mrs Lawrence," Geoff said.

"Come and sit down, then," Mrs Smith said, opening the door of the communal sitting room where they had been before. "What about Mrs Lawrence?" she asked and added, "Dr Harris, isn't it? Wasn't it you that gave evidence at the inquest on that man they found in a cellar in Meadowfield?"

"So you read the account? Only my name didn't appear in the press, you know. In fact the inquest on that man they found was adjourned, because there had been no identification. But wasn't it, mustn't it, have been the man you told us was James Lawrence, Mrs Lawrence's husband?"

"She called him Jim."

Lucy said, "You knew, didn't you, that she was married to old Mr Lawrence?"

"Are you calling me a liar?"

The doorbell, pressed by an energetic hand, pealed through the house. There was silence in the room while the girl in the overall opened the front door to the new visitor.

"She's got people with her," they heard her say.

"My friends. I've come to join them."

Mrs Smith sprang up, fear in her eyes, her face whitening. "What the bloody hell — "

"Ah," Mr Lawrence said, pausing in the doorway, the girl holding the door open, supreme indifference in her face and manner, "Have Geoff and Lucy told you who I am?" He turned to them, "No? She hasn't been told yet? Well, Mrs Smith, that is the name, I believe. I have just come from Dorothy's employers and they told me she had a bed-sitter here for over a year when she was working with them. Before she married my father."

The blood rushed back into Mrs Smith's face. She had been standing, but she dropped back into her chair, choking, gasping, and searching for her handkerchief.

"You knew that I was in England, didn't you? And of course you knew perfectly well that the man who came here and spent the night with my stepmother was not her husband, but her lover."

Mrs Smith licked her dry lips but said nothing.

"I expect the police have been here to ask questions about him, haven't they? I'm not interested in the rotten bastard, or his unpleasant death. But I do want to know the truth about that short visit of my father. Had he stayed with you before?"

"No. He hadn't. But he came to the house to take Dot out when he was courting her."

James Lawrence's face twisted at thought of this picture.

"I know he booked two rooms for himself. I have seen his letter."

Mrs Smith darted a venomous look at Geoff, who smiled and shrugged in return.

"Research my foot!" she hissed.

"Research of a forensic kind," he answered. "Very valuable, as it happens."

"He booked two rooms," repeated Mr Lawrence, "so I imagine he knew that his wife was having an affair and had stopped sleeping with her. You knew that already, too, didn't you?"

Mrs Smith said nothing.

"So when this Jim character arrived it is hardly surprising that my father blew his top. And threw him out, perhaps?"

"They quarrelled," said Mrs Smith. "The old gentleman was very abusive and Jim was upset, but Dot got between them and persuaded him to go. I said he was not to come back, because they were shouting and upsetting my other gentlemen."

"But he did come back, didn't he?" Geoff interrupted. "You said before that he spent the night with his wife. Was that partly true or a complete lie?"

"I'm not speaking to *you*," said Mrs Smith, glaring at him.

"The real point is," Mr Lawrence insisted, taking firm control again, "from what you say my father suffered quite enough upset and indignity to push his blood pressure well above the danger point in a man of seventy. Don't you agree, doctor?"

"Quite possible, but you couldn't prove it."

"What I can't understand," said Lucy, speaking for the first time since Mr Lawrence's arrival, "is why you had to invent all that about the other man being James Lawrence, when we came before."

"You can mind your own business, miss," returned Mrs Smith tartly.

"I suppose the big brute threatened — " Geoff began, but Mr Lawrence checked him.

"I don't think we need keep Mrs Smith any longer," he said. "Come along, you two. Thank you, madam," he went on, as they moved down the hall to the front door. "I'm afraid you are in for some more shocks beyond anything the police have already told you."

"They haven't told me anything," she answered, subdued now and beginning to be tearful. "Just asked questions on and on and warned me not to keep anything from them."

"Such as?"

"Her whereabouts if she does get on to me."

"Good advice," Geoff could not help endorsing.

"As for you, young man," she retorted, her voice rising shrilly, "you and your floosie. You call yourself a doctor. Doctor, I don't think, nor her neither."

"Physio," corrected Lucy. It was automatic and said quietly, but it angered Mrs Smith beyond endurance and her right hand lifted to smack.

"Nasty temper!" Mr Lawrence said, holding the hand motionless in mid air until Mrs Smith dropped it with an audible sob and retreated, slamming the door.

"My poor father," said Mr Lawrence sadly, looking up at the dingy house before he turned away.

The three of them were very quiet on the way back. Mr Lawrence drove, with Geoff beside him to pilot him out of Lincoln and through the approaches to Meadowfield. He dropped the two young people at the surgery, apologising for not giving them a meal before they parted

"That's all right," Lucy told him. "I don't think any of us feel much like food yet. I'm so very sorry it turned out so — so sordid."

"Thank you, my dear," Mr Lawrence said and drove away.

As Lucy had guessed he did not want a meal yet, though it was well into the afternoon and he had had an early breakfast. He drove to the Social Services building and demanded to see Mrs Chandler at once. This time Beryl came to him in the waiting room to say she would be free in five minutes.

Immediately on entering her room Lawrence saw that she had been diminished. The stiff upright presence behind the wide desk was replaced by a seemingly shorter torso, a less prominent bosom, with above it a face in which fear and obstinacy fought for over-all control.

Mr Lawrence sat down without invitation and gave Mrs Chandler a detailed account of his visit to Lincoln, including a few details about Dorothy, his stepmother, that he had not recounted to Mrs Smith because Geoff and Lucy were there and he saw no point in boosting their already well-founded disapproval of her..

"So you see I was right in criticising the lack of thoroughness of your department in assessing, as you call it, Mrs Lawrence."

"I don't accept that," Mrs Chandler said and shut her lips into a thin line of denial.

"You'll have to, I'm afraid. The police have been there, too. They know that she was dismissed from the agricultural supplies firm for suspected, but not proved, dishonesty and took advantage of my poor father's infatuation to prod him into marriage."

"Suspicion is not proof, it is more usually prejudice," Mrs Chandler said, rallying. "Mrs Lawrence, I am sure, was genuinely appalled by the action of the firm in dismissing her out of hand, with no appeal. And so was Mrs Smith. Your father's affection and his admirable compassion saved her from great unpleasantness, if not danger."

Mrs Chandler, rolling these well-worn sentiments from her ever-ready tongue, seemed to revive with their delivery. She sat up straighter, took hold of a pencil on her desk and tapped with it on Mrs Lawrence's file, open before her.

"So you knew about her past five years ago with the firm in Lincoln, did you?" Mr Lawrence asked.

"No, I did *not*. I know the facts from Dorothy Lawrence herself and from Mrs Smith to whom she referred me."

"*Facts!* Has it never occurred to you, Mrs Chandler, that she may have lied to you? That both women lied to you? You help to administer public money, don't you? Do you employ *any* safeguards?"

Mrs Chandler was wilting again now, but her obstinacy was growing.

"I believe my clients until I have proof of their unworthiness," she insisted. "I believe in my own judgment after a good many years of experience."

"Then God help you!" said Mr Lawrence, his temper, never quiescent for long, rising rapidly. "At least you must agree that she deceived you over her relationship with my father and with the very doubtful character she called Jim? Even Mrs Smith didn't know, or wouldn't say, who he was, except that I think the police have matched him with the corpse we found at The Old Farmhouse."

"That is none of my business," said Mrs Chandler.

Mr Lawrence saw no reason to dispute this. Beryl saw him out of the Social Services office, giving a wink and a shrug to Margery at the telephones that worried that hard-working young woman for quite five minutes.

The police in the persons of Detective Chief Inspector Bartlet and Detective Sergeant Pearce had indeed sorted out Mrs Smith with the approval and aid of the Lincoln force, in a second interview on the day after Mr Lawrence's visit. Taken together, Mrs Smith's two accounts matched in all essentials. Both men were very agreeably content with the result of their second interview, which included much the landlady had so far withheld.

Mrs Lawrence, as Dorothy Wilson, had rented a bedsitter at the guest house for nearly two years before she lost her job with the agricultural supplies firm. She had met Mr Lawrence at the firm's offices, where she worked in the accounts department. She had confided, in a jokey sort of way, Mrs Smith said, that the old goat fancied her and had taken her out to dinner at his hotel before getting his night train home to the north. Her dismissal had been a nasty knock, but it happened just before Mr Lawrence made another visit to Lincoln. It appeared he had not forgotten her, for he came to the guest house, very upset to find her in trouble. Naturally she made the most of it. Well, any girl would, Mrs Smith argued, seeing her references had gone and she had no family, all dead, she had always said, and no future. Mr Lawrence was prepared to give her one and she took it. Not all that romantic, but at the time he looked far younger than he was and he was a kind gentleman. He never showed his real temper as he did that last night before his stroke.

"So there actually was a quarrel then?" Bartlet asked.

"My God, was there not! Blew up like a bomb the instant Jim set foot in the house. Real nasty temper like that son of his has, judging by what he acted like when he was here yesterday."

"Young Lawrence was here, was he?"

"With the doctor and the girl that calls herself a — "

"Physio?" suggested Detective Sergeant Pearce.

"Whatever that is, when it's at home."

"Physiotherapist," Bartlet explained. "She treated old Mr Lawrence to the best of her ability. But it's this character Jim we want to ask you about. What's his full name?"

"That I never knew," Mrs Smith answered. "But they'd

known each other for years, he and Dot. As good as married, you understand."

The detectives said they understood perfectly. By a tortuous and time-consuming route they also discovered that Jim had been in the habit of coming to see Dorothy every month or so at weekends. She had given him a small room of his own for these visits, but he had never slept there, not even bothered to rumple up the sheets, though Dorothy's bed on those occasions provided all the evidence for a divorce, if the gentlemen took her meaning, which again they did.

It was not until Mr Lawrence had been found on the floor of his room that Jim, after phoning for the ambulance, had told her that he was James Lawrence, son of the old gentleman and that Dot was his wife.

"Which you knew darned well and had known for years was a lie," Bartlet accused.

Mrs Smith hesitated, shaken but not really afraid.

"if you'd known Jim as well as I did by then you wouldn't have wanted to dispute anything he told you," she said at last. "He as much as said if I opened my mouth to anyone he'd burn the guest house to the ground with me in it."

"So why are you telling us all that now?"

"Because he's dead, isn't he?"

Mrs Smith stared at them, appalled by the possibility of Jim's continued existence.

"That's what we think," said the Detective Chief Inspector, smiling at her. "We hope you will confirm it by picking out any photograph you recognise from this selection. You must tell us, Mrs Smith, if you have ever seen any one of these men before."

He handed her a neatly stacked series of six police photographs. They came from the records of old lags; six sinister looking thugs who had served prison sentences of varying lengths and at varying intervals over the last twenty years.

"That's Jim," said Mrs Smith. "Not but what he's older now and his hair's longer and a beard."

"It was longer and he did have a four days beard when we saw him dead in The Old Farmhouse cellar," Detective Sergeant Pearce told her, earning a frown from Bartlet.

"I'd like you to make us a statement, please, Mrs Smith. You definitely identify the man you know as Jim with the picture and the number given on that photograph?"

"I do," said Mrs Smith, "and I will put in my statement that the miserable bastard threatened me if I didn't tell everyone he was Mr James Lawrence and the husband of Mrs Dorothy Lawrence."

But she did not ask, and they did not tell her, who Jim really was. Nor the length of time he had been known to the police, chiefly in the Midlands, but further north as well. Nor that the corpse had been identified already by its fingerprints as the known criminal James Binscott, suspected of yet another brutal murder in the course of robbery, and on the run, with the police totally mystified until his body turned up, a very welcome present on a most interesting plate, in the cellar at Meadowfield.

13

ABOUT A WEEK later Margery, mechanically working at the telephone exchange of the Meadowfield Social Services, heard a voice she recognised. Automatically she gave the name of the establishment, following it with the standard question, "Can I help you?"

"I want to speak to Mrs Chandler," the voice said.

"And the name, please?"

"Mrs Chandler."

"*Your* name, please, madam."

Margery felt she knew it already, but there was something about the clipped way the caller had asked for Mrs Chandler, ordered it, rather, that put the girl off. Could she have been mistaken?

Getting no answer she asked once more for a name to put through to Mrs Chandler.

"Dorothy," said the caller. "Dorothy Wilson. Just put me through to Mrs Chandler's room. Don't waste time getting Beryl."

Obviously she was mistaken, Margery decided. She could have sworn it was Mrs Lawrence. She spoke to Beryl on the houseline. The latter said, "Do what she wants. I'll take it as well on the extension."

Without warning their superior, the two girls then listened to a brief but intriguing conversation.

"Is that Mrs Chandler?"

"Yes. Surely? Well, what a surprise! Where are you?"

"I must speak to you. It's Dorothy."

"I know it's Dorothy. Did you think I wouldn't recognise your voice?"

"Dorothy Wilson," said the caller. "I must speak to you, but perhaps — "

"Listen," said Mrs Chandler firmly. "We are very busy here, as always. I take it this is a personal problem you want to consult me about. I suggest you give me a telephone number where I can find you later today. About six, say. Between six and seven."

"I'll ring you," the answer came. "I'd rather. If you'll give me your home number. *Please!*"

Mrs Chandler was most unwilling to let the office have her private number. She had kept it ex-directory, ever since her husband had walked out on her. Only head office knew it, together with the address of the house. But she knew the voice of the caller; she had recognised it immediately. So she must certainly listen to what Dorothy Lawrence — Wilson, indeed — had to say to her. The most interesting and worthwhile client she had had for a very long time.

Speaking in a low voice, almost a whisper, that she imagined Beryl, even if she were listening in, might not hear, she gave her private number, said in a louder voice, "about seven, Dorothy," and rang off.

"That was Mrs Lawrence, wasn't it?" Beryl remarked when she brought Mrs Chandler her mid-morning cup of coffee.

"What was Mrs Lawrence?" the latter asked coldly.

"That call the client said she was Dorothy Wilson."

"How do *you* know she called herself Dorothy Wilson?" Beryl was not disturbed.

"Because Margery told me on the house phone. She was thrilled — Margery, I mean. After all these weeks and that body turning up really scarey and — "

"That will do, Beryl," Mrs Chandler was pale with rage. "The death at The Old Farmhouse, after Mrs Lawrence

127

had left; some tramp I suppose, taking shelter from the storm; all that, is no business of ours and none of hers, I expect. I sincerely hope not, anyway."

Beryl looked at her boss with awe and some reluctant admiration. Did she *never* read the newspapers or look at the news? There had been a lot of speculation, but nothing so utterly off-beam as Mrs Chandler's scatty suggestions.

The two girls compared notes at the end of the day, concluding that it looked as if Mrs Lawrence was in some sort of fresh trouble for herself this time and that Mrs Chandler was more likely to make it worse than better.

"Look what happened at Seacombe," Beryl reminded Margery.

"I don't see that was anybody's fault."

"She persuaded Mrs Lawrence to take him down there. Turned out to be her old hubby, didn't he?"

"What did Mrs Chandler have to say to that?"

"Nothing. I daren't mention it."

"Why ever not?"

"Look," said Beryl firmly. "I'm not in this lark for the fun of it. Who would be? Half the staff are nut-cases themselves or queer. But I'm out to get something better, see, and that means a good word from our Violet."

"O.K., O.K.," interrupted Margery. "You needn't tell me. I wouldn't be still in Meadowfield myself if my mum wasn't so stuck on not moving out. Kid brother likes his present teacher and never plays truant any more. Or so she thinks."

"Then you agree we've got to butter up Violet, if we can?"

"Oh, sure."

"Did you put down that call as Wilson or Lawrence?"

"Half a sec. Yes, Wilson."

"Same here. Wilson it is, in spite of what we know it was that all-time twister, Lawrence. Dorothy Wilson, personal call to Mrs Chandler. And we've got Violet's home number, for what it's worth."

"I won't forget, Beryl," her friend assured her.

The call came to Mrs Chandler's bungalow at eight o'clock that evening, interrupting her enjoyment on television of a solemn illustrated lecture on the danger and disablement at work of public lamplighters in the early years of the century, compared and contrasted with the risks and sufferings from cancer in the asbestos factories of the present day.

She lifted the receiver in a spirit of resentment.

"Am I speaking to Mrs Chandler?" a cautious voice inquired.

"Yes, Dorothy, you are."

"Oh, Violet, I am in such trouble I had to ring you. You aren't angry with me?"

The call for help, for guidance, was irresistible.

"No, of course not. But why couldn't you explain at the office? I mean, why pretend your name was Wilson? It didn't deceive me, nor Margery, I'm sure."

Mrs Lawrence's voice, answering the charge, was more than ever her own, crisp, quiet, self-assured. "And I'm sure you knew, at once. Wilson is my maiden name. I have gone back to it because my husband, just before his stroke, made a new will, leaving everything to his son, cutting me out entirely, in spite of all I did for him in the five years of our marriage."

"Your marriage. Yes." Mrs Chandler, struggling to relate this fresh complaint with all she knew, or thought she knew, of her client, could not resist a justified complaint of her own. "You should have told me about it, Dorothy. Right from the beginning. You allowed us all to think —"

"I never said he wasn't my husband. I never said, never once, that Jim was his son, or that he was my husband."

"But he is, isn't he?" Mrs Chandler was by now utterly confused. "I mean, wasn't he? No, of course not. How could he be? Old Mr Lawrence was your husband, you have just said so. But Jim —"

"Was a great friend of mine at one time," Mrs Lawrence said, with a pathetic little catch in her voice. "It was to escape from his influence, really, that I allowed Mr Lawrence to take me out, and then to marry me."

"But surely this Jim was the man that the real Mr James Lawrence and that estate agent found dead at The Old Farmhouse? That was this Jim of yours, wasn't he? He came to see you, didn't he?"

There was a little pause, then Mrs Lawrence said, in a very cautious tone, "Is that what they are all saying?"

Here was a frightened, muddled woman, Mrs Chandler told herself. She must proceed very gently, not frighten her further. No good to tell her to go to the police. They would bully her, torture her with questions, if not blows. She knew the police.

"Dorothy," she said, in the voice that Mrs Lawrence always thought was enough to make her throw up, "my dear, did Jim, I mean, was it Jim, who visited you on the Sunday night of the thunderstorm in Meadowfield? Everything you tell me is in strict confidence, you know that."

Of course I know, why else do you think I'm ringing you at home, you bloody silly cow, Mrs Lawrence thought, but she said slowly and regretfully, "Yes, I'm afraid it was Jim. I had told him I had to leave The Old Farmhouse because it was left to James Lawrence and so was Hillside Farm. He was very, very angry."

"And then?" Mrs Chandler waited eagerly for the true story of that night.

"He wouldn't listen to reason. I was frightened of him. I thought he would kill me. So I took a few of my things and left."

"So you didn't know — ? You don't know — ?"

"I only know that I travelled in the early hours to Penrith and Hillside Farm was locked up, too, and I phoned a friend and she took me in."

Poor woman, poor woman, thought Mrs Chandler, just

one calamity after another. Not surprising she isn't always quite straight. But her present circumstances seem clear enough.

"Where are you now, Dorothy?" she asked, breaking into the flow of misfortune.

"With my friend." Mrs Lawrence paused, then went on with her carefully prepared request. "I wonder, Violet," she said. "I have several friends near Manchester. I wonder if you could put me on to the Social Services people there? You've been so good to me at Meadowfield and over Seacombe. Would there be anyone in Manchester?"

Mrs Chandler wrestled madly with her memory, trying to force it to disclose a name, man or woman, of a contemporary who now worked in that great conurbation.

"Yes," she said, triumphant at last. "Archie Hill. Archibald Hill. Let me see, he was near Fallowfield at one time. Now — well, I don't know where he works now, but you can enquire. I'm sure he must be in some senior position. Hill, the name is, Archibald."

"I've got that. Thanks so much." Mrs Lawrence sounded pleased, perhaps a little breathless.

"Let me know how — " Mrs Chandler began, but she heard the bell ring that ended the call and replaced her own receiver sadly. Clients. Even the nice ones, like poor Dorothy, were seldom really grateful and their manners, these days, were often wanting. She would have liked to warn Dorothy about the interest the Law was taking in her. As if she could tell them anything when she had left the house before that man, whom she had confessed was her Jim, had fallen into the cellar. Well, if the police found her they would ask their own questions. It was not her business to help them. Manchester. Was that where the friend lived who had taken her in? Not Penrith or Carlisle? Well, she had rung off rather abruptly, hadn't she? Before giving her address or even a telephone number, so there were no means of getting in touch with

131

her. And certainly nothing to report at the office. Nothing at all.

"Another call from the coroner," Detective Sergeant Pearce announced, following Detective Chief Inspector Bartlet into his room at the police station. "Wants to fix a definite date for renewal of the inquest on Binscott."

"He does, does he?" Bartlet growled. "Tell him he can have a definite identification, but we still haven't got the chief witness."

"Meaning Mrs Lawrence?"

"Naturally. She appears to have been there when it happened, so accident, if that's correct, seems strange."

"Because she didn't try to get help when he fell into the cellar?"

"Not only that but the question of the ladder. Why wasn't it in the proper place? Why and by whom had it been doctored and why had he not been warned?"

"Proper booby trap, wasn't it? Just needed two hands on the top rails and one step forward and the whole thing would collapse."

"Sideways as we found it."

"So he must have put the light on before he fell?"

"Not necessarily. But she must have turned it off again or why wasn't it on when Lawrence and Stone found themselves on the edge of the drop.

"And she must have locked the cellar door on the outside. All that after the poor devil had fallen and she was doing nothing to help him."

"We'll have a job to prove any of it. Can you see any jury finding her capable of sawing off that ladder at the right spot and the right depth to make it collapse when stepped on?"

They were silent, each trying to reconstruct the possible behaviour of a determined would-be murderess and a violent experienced murderer.

At last Bartlet said, "She could have doctored the ladder

leaving the top step and handles balanced at the top and the ladder already pushed away. Then if Binscott opened the door, saw what he took for the ladder in the light from the hall and went in, reaching for the light switch — "

"He could fall in the dark." Pearce nodded agreement. "That's much more likely, isn't it, sir?"

"I would think so. But I still don't see a jury wearing it. Or even the coroner."

"We didn't find a saw of any sort whatever at The Old Farmhouse, did we, sir?"

"No. Nor her fingerprints anywhere on the ladder or in the cellar."

"But they were on that piece of old tin she must have propped up on purpose over the cellar window to keep out the light."

"Or stop anyone looking in."

"That too, I suppose."

"We've only got what we think are her prints in the bedroom she was using, or we think she was using."

Again they sat thinking until Detective Sergeant Pearce said, "About her clothes. That anorak the people saw on the character leaving in the early hours next day. Would that be Jim coming and her going? If we're right, I mean?"

"Very likely," Bartlet agreed.

"Cold-blooded bitch," said Pearce.

"She's that all right if we're nailing it all on the right person."

"There's still the garden snooper," suggested Pearce, encouraged by his superior's indulgence. "Do we know where the rumour about him came from?"

"We do not," said Detective Chief Inspector Bartlet, rousing himself and tearing up a page of inappropriate doodles. "We do not, but you can make it your business to run him down and bring him to me and you can try the landlord of The Sitting Duck first and that promising snooper and public nuisance, young Tine."

"Sir," said Detective Sergeant Pearce.

14

ARCHIBALD HILL RECEIVED Dorothy Lawrence, née Wilson, with strong misgivings. In her letter to him Violet Chandler, whom he remembered by name only, had described this individual as 'such a nice client, but so dreadfully unfortunate'. Dreadful indeed was the history Mrs Chandler related in a short resumé from her file, and most unfortunate, employing that word in all its various uses, past and present.

But when Mrs Lawrence appeared, ushered into his room by his middle-aged, stout secretary, he felt a distinctly pleasurable shock of surprise. For he had expected a down-trodden, querulous woman, whose present unhappy position was the result of stupidity, and that familiar type of dishonesty born of fear. Instead he saw a handsome, well-dressed, even fashionably dressed, person. She had carefully trimmed and waved hair, moderate make-up that did not hide, but softened the mature facial lines of an early middle-aged face, and an expression that was anxious but showed no sign of defeat.

"Mrs Lawrence?" he asked, directing her to the chair beside his flat-topped, knee-hole desk.

"Wilson," she answered. "My maiden name. I have gone back to it because — because — "

She began to fumble for a handkerchief.

"Mrs Chandler sent me a report," Mr Hill said, hurriedly, to forestall tears. He never allowed tears in his private office: too disturbing, too dangerous. "In that she tells me that you were married to a man very much older than yourself, who is now dead, due to an accident, having previously suffered a disabling stroke. Also that prior to the stroke he altered his will, so that he left his whole estate away from you, owing to — er — alleged misbehaviour on your part. No, let me finish. Mrs Chandler puts 'alleged' in her letter. She says you reverted to your maiden name, partly in shock and anger at this treatment by your husband — "

Mrs Lawrence succeeded at last in breaking into what she considered Violet's long-winded saga. "I looked after him *for five whole years*!"

"Yes," said Mr Hill. He was used to interruptions and usually disregarded them if they did not match or enlarge his own conclusions. "That is understandable. But not legal, you know. Your marriage was legal, I take it?"

"Of course."

"And you may not know it, but probably you are entitled to some legacy, notwithstanding the will. A wife may not be disinherited entirely, as a rule. Though Mrs Chandler — "

"I went back to the name Wilson," Mrs Lawrence interrupted again. "partly to avoid the press. They've been awful. At Seacombe, that's where the accident happened, and at Meadowfield and Penrith and Carlisle, after that body was found — "

"The body," insisted Mr Hill, interrupting in his turn and very forcefully this time. "Mrs Chandler suggests — but I should like you to tell me what you know of this person. This man who was found dead at The Old Farmhouse. Was it he your husband objected to?"

Mrs Lawrence nodded. The handkerchief she had ready might be needed quite soon now. She swallowed once or twice. This man was very insistent. He was going to worm it all out of her if she let out more than was safe. At present anyhow. She allowed her eyes to fill slowly, then said, "I won't deny it. I mustn't, must I? But Jim was the sort that never lets go. We — we'd been very good friends, well, intimate, before I met Mr Lawrence. I knew him up here, at my friend's where I'm staying now. When Mr Lawrence wanted to marry me I already was longing to break with Jim, but dared not tell him. I didn't really love Mr Lawrence then, he was so much older than me — "

"How old are you, Mrs — er — Wilson?"

"Thirty-five." She hoped that was what she had told Mrs Chandler and was relieved to see from Mr Hill's rapid check with the letter before him, that she had remembered correctly.

"So you were thirty when you married and he, your husband, was sixty-five. It was a risk, wasn't it?"

Mrs Lawrence ventured a wan smile.

"He was very good to me."

"But Jim came after you?"

"It was hell on earth, Mr Hill. For those five years I had to fight him off. He rang up at all hours, he came to the farm, Hillside, where we lived. He threatened me. I thought at one time he'd given up, but not a bit of it."

"Did you tell your husband about this persecution?"

"Oh, yes. He was angry at first because I hadn't told him before we were married. But he was very understanding. Until Jim followed us to Lincoln and made a dreadful scene. And that upset Mr Lawrence and I think it brought on his stroke."

Time for a breakdown now, Mrs Lawrence decided, before I say too much about Jim. She buried her face in her handkerchief and began to sob in a very heart-broken manner.

This was a mistake, for if there was one thing that upset Archie Hill to the point of destroying his sympathy, it was tears. So now he jumped up, pressing his hand on the bell for his secretary and when the stout Mrs Lone appeared said, "Mrs Wilson is upset. Tell her to call again tomorrow morning," left the room and did not come back.

136

Bastard, Mrs Lawrence told herself, sipping tea at a nearby café. She began to plan her revenge for the delay in organising her means of support. That evening she confided the plan to Rosie Lord who had proved herself a true friend and in whose present house she was staying.

Hearing the plan Rosie smacked her knee and laughed heartily.

"Back to old times, eh? I take my hat off, I do really, Dot."

With her head on one side she regarded her old friend seriously, critically, professionally, but with amused kindliness.

"Think he'll play up?" she asked. "He must know your age, doesn't he?"

"I told him thirty-five."

"You can bring that down to thirty if your figure's good enough."

"It'll have to be."

"But is he the type?"

Mrs Lawrence considered.

"He liked what he saw until I began to cry. Can't stand women blubbing, his fat secretary told me."

"Fat? If that's how he likes them you haven't a chance in hell, dear."

Mrs Lawrence laughed.

"How do we know he chose her? She may have been wished on him to guarantee no complications." She paused. "That's an idea," she said. "He used to work out Fallowfield way, Violet Chandler told me. I wonder why he was moved up here?"

"Promotion?"

"Or the opposite. Could you find out for me, Rosie? You always know all the local dirt. Be a sport. I'm getting desperate, I really am. Not a word from those damned solicitors."

"But they know you've left Meadowfield and Hillside.

137

What address can they use, if you haven't given them one?"

"I've paid the Post Office to send them on here." She saw Rosie's face grow red and hastened to add, "For the next six weeks only."

"It had better be only, my girl. It's my livelihood, have you forgotten?"

"Of course not. Oh, Rosie," said Mrs Lawrence, with every appearance of sincerity, "you are good to me!"

The house where Miss Lord was now living and where she offered massage and kindred services on little cards stuck on the glass doors of local newsagents, was a larger and more important dwelling than the flat that she had shared with Dot in the old days. Then they had both been call-girls, in partnership for the rent and rates, the lighting, heating and telephone. It was over seven years since Dot began to feel her girlish appeal was weakening and so had answered the advertisement for a responsible post in Lincoln. And got it too, in spite of what should have been quite obvious deficiencies in knowledge, skill and all the other attributes of a secretary in a big finance department. With Jim's help in the way of references, of course. There wasn't much he hadn't known about finance, nor Dot about men. She had helped Jim in several very tricky transactions before Lincoln, Rosie was sure.

On the whole she was not too pleased to have Dot back. Certainly she felt very uneasy over the present development. But her innate laziness and good nature got the better of experience. Besides, she only ran the house now for the benefit of her girls, renting the separate rooms to individuals and providing hot drinks and frozen meals on a very meagre scale. If they wanted alcohol they had to buy it for themselves and bring it in themselves. She didn't want to know.

On the next two successive days Mrs Lawrence attended the Social Services offices, usually seeing Mr Hill, to fill up various forms under his instruction and while doing so to continue her reminiscences of life at Hillside Farm with Mr Lawrence, pursued by the man, Jim.

Mrs Lawrence presented a quiet, dignified, but not very intelligent picture of bereavement and bewilderment at her unaccustomed financial stress. Mr Hill began to enjoy his position of power over her affairs. He had always liked to feel superior to women, to exercise power over them of one kind or another. Never a sadistic power; his impulses were always tender.

It distressed him, therefore, when he read in his national newspaper an account of the re-opened inquest on the 'corpse in the cellar' at Meadowfield. He took the paper with him to the office and when Mrs Lawrence was shown into his room for the third morning running, he first directed her to the chair beside his desk, then placing his finger on the opened page of *Home News* said "You have no doubt read this piece, Mrs Wilson."

"No, I don't think so," she answered, leaning forward.

He turned the page towards her, holding the sheet flat. She pulled her chair closer to the desk. She had un-buttoned her jacket and now, pushing it still further open, so as not to obstruct her view, her figure, particularly that feature known as the 'cleavage' became very obvious to Mr Hill. He was disturbed, so much so that in his mounting excitement he did not notice his client's equally severe disturbance, though from an entirely different cause.

For Mrs Lawrence had seen the picture of a familiar face and below it the name James Binscott. Beside and above the photograph was the story told to the coroner by a number of witnesses.

Feverishly she scanned the account for the fatal, the dangerous clues, but they did not appear. The inquest was again adjourned.

Mrs Lawrence lifted a white face and terrified eyes to Mr Hill. Her fear and shock, being perfectly genuine, produced in him an added flood of emotion. He stammered, "My dear Mrs Lawrence! My poor — "

He was checked only by her collapse forward, across the newspaper, sideways across the desk, sideways from her chair into his ready, willing arms. From this position her weight pulled him from his own chair so that they sank to the floor together in a tangled heap.

Mr Hill in his turn was now a frightened man. As gently as he could he pulled himself away from Mrs Lawrence and then prudently pulled Mrs Lawrence away from her close proximity to his desk. After straightening his clothes and his papers on the desk he rang for Mrs Lone.

She came at once, by which time Mrs Lawrence was moaning slightly and moving her head from side to side.

"She fainted quite suddenly," Mr Hill explained. "No, don't let her get up yet. First-aid, you know."

"What upset her?" asked Mrs Lone, who was knowledgeable enough to feel for the sufferer's pulse and found it full and bounding, if still rapid.

"A paragraph in the paper," said Mr Hill. "Stay with her, please, Mrs Lone, until she is fit to leave. I will go and arrange for a taxi to get her home."

"Where's that?" asked Mrs Lone. "We've got no local address for her, have we?"

Mrs Lawrence murmured something in a faint voice.

"What did you say, dear?" Mrs Lone, on her knees, bent nearer. "Number Three, Fothergill Mansions," she reported, looking up at Mr Hill.

He repeated it and left the room, while Mrs Lawrence slowly recovered, cursing herself for this mismanaged part of the act.

A few minutes later the house phone in Mr Hill's room ordered Mrs Lone to take the client, if sufficiently recovered, to the front hall of the building where a pre-paid taxi was waiting to drive her home. The voice giving these instructions was Mr Hill's, but he was not present in the hall when the two women arrived there.

Mrs Lawrence cursed herself again for overplaying her part. Mrs Lone, knowing her principal's former history in

140

the Social Service was inclined to admire his present caution. She saw Mrs Lawrence, still wan and weak, drive away, then returned at once to her duty. Having written down the address she had given to the taxi driver, she put it away in her private handbag before making sure that Mr Hill was back in his office.

He in his turn had both heard and remembered the faint words spoken by his client. He, also, had written down her address, for surely it was his duty in spite of — no, because of — his position to make sure Dorothy Lawrence was not suffering too cruelly from the relentless blows of ill-fortune that continued to assail her. There was really only one way to do this without driving himself silly waiting for her to come again to his office. He would go along to Fothergill Mansions, wherever they hung out, and make certain her friend was taking proper care of her.

Common sense, common prudence, screamed at him to forbear. He was not a complete bloody fool, he told himself. Mrs Lone had the address too. Officially, it should be attached to Dorothy's file. He took the precaution at the end of the day, when the secretaries had gone home, to see if Mrs Lone had added it. She had not. So much the better. She would soon forget. Her memory for names and addresses was markedly poor. Without the computer life would be far harder than it was. Tomorrow, Mr Hill thought, tomorrow he would go to enquire. He would move carefully, slowly, at his age nothing else was suitable. And after all, she was not a girl, though wonderfully preserved. He remembered, in a shuddering wave of longing, the way her head had fallen to his shoulder and her soft breast, escaping from her bra, lay under his hand before they had collapsed on to the floor together.

The next day Mr Hill carried out his plan. He told Mrs Lone he would be visiting in the afternoon. This was not unheard of, though he had not had many urgent cases recently, or not those he felt needed checking because they seemed to make no progress.

Mrs Lone, taking instructions for his absence, sighed a little, but decided to wait. She was there to give him stability, she told herself, remembering her interview with the head of the department. So far there had been no trouble. It must stay that way.

Mr Hill saw two of his more difficult clients at their own homes before driving on to Fothergill Mansions in a part of his district that was unfamiliar to him. However, he was agreeably surprised to find the building old-fashioned but not dilapidated. In fact it had been painted fairly recently and stood out, pale grey and white, from its more dingy neighbours. Mr Hill was so pleasantly surprised by this spruceness that he failed to notice the colour of the lamp hanging in the wide porch, half hidden by the surrounding pillars, until he was standing just below it, looking at a panel of names and bell pushes.

Was it a delicate shade of pink? He shrugged off the implications. All the name cards were feminine, but what of that? Wilson was not among them, nor Lawrence. But Dorothy was staying with a friend, she had said, whose name was Rosie. No surname. Try 'Caretaker.'

This succeeded. 'Caretaker' was Rosie herself and Dorothy was at home.

"Come right in," said Rosie, smiling. "Mr Hill, did you say?"

He had not said it, merely asked for Mrs Wilson, but he understood that this was Dorothy's friend, with whom she was staying. And it was a call-girl establishment. More refined than a brothel, but from Rosie's appearance and manner, much the same thing.

Without correcting her he merely said he had come from the Social Service Offices to enquire after Mrs Wilson, who had been taken ill there the day before.

"Much better," Rosie said. "I'm sure she'd like to tell you so herself."

It was much easier than he had expected. So easy, so simple, that he found himself in Dorothy's room before

142

he had time to realise how thoroughly he had given himself away. She told him how sorry she was for collapsing in his office and how she had dared to hope he would call, just to enquire. It was wonderful actually to see him in the flesh.

She giggled a little as she said 'flesh', letting the long soft robe she was wearing — one of Rosie's — fall away a little to reveal, through transparent nylon, far more of that enchanting flesh that had so bemused Mr Hill in their collapse together the day before.

By now he was beyond doubt or caution, making up for a long abstinence with a thoroughness that Mrs Lawrence found tedious, though she was far too professional to allow him any doubt of her equal enjoyment. It was not until he left the house a couple of hours later, restored by tea laced with brandy — disgusting drink Rosie said to Dot, shuddering — that he drove only a short distance before pulling up in a lay-by, to allow his heart to stop its renewed wild thumping, his mind to calm its terror and his hands to grip the controls without shaking.

He did not go back to the office that day. Mrs Lone waited for him until the caretaker came up to see why she was still there.

"He's out visiting," she explained. "Several cases. I had an important message for him. Trunk call."

"He'll have gone straight home without calling back," the caretaker suggested.

"I hope so," Mrs Lone said, stiffly.

"You could ring him there if it's important," the man said. "From your own place, I mean. I've got to lock up here, now."

"Be your age," said Mrs Lone, crossly, pulling the cover over her typewriter.

But she kept wondering what that long-distance call was about from Mrs Chandler at Meadowfield. The woman was making it in person and would not speak to anyone but Mr Hill. It was about that client Lawrence, Mrs

Dorothy Lawrence or Wilson. It would be, Mrs Lone told herself, fishing in her handbag for the bit of paper on which she had written that deceitful client's address. Poor dear Archie! No match for them, was he? She'd have to have a go again: save him from himself. The powers that be would never wear another turn-up like the last.

15

MADE CARELESS BY her success in the seduction of Archie Hill, Mrs Lawrence allowed herself to prolong her night's rest a little. She woke at her usual hour, but turned over and let herself doze away into half dreams of a future life free from worry, where money spilled into her purse without effort and no unpleasant threats hung over her: where she could plan her future in safety, without having the plan destroyed almost as soon as it was made.

Rosie looked into her room at a little past nine, but as her friend did not move or speak, shut the door again softly, to return downstairs to her kitchen to enjoy her own breakfast of toast and good, strong tea. Also her newspaper, in which she found a short paragraph that sent her upstairs again soon to rouse Dot with certain disturbing news.

By this time Mrs Lawrence, who had heard Rosie come in the first time, had decided it was time to begin a new day. She had roused herself to the point of sitting up in bed, wondering how to pass the time until her next appointment with Archie, when her door opened again. She saw Rosie's face and the way she waved the newspaper she carried. She guessed that something disagreeable had happened. The half dreams vanished as usual.

"Give it here," she demanded. "Whereabouts? What is it?"

"There," Rosie told her, pointing. " 'Police find in cellar case.' Doesn't say what. Can you guess, Dot?"

"Of course not. How could I?"

Watching her read it Rosie had no doubt whatever that it was something Dot knew very well and that her present use of the room she occupied might be not only inconvenient, but even dangerous. Dot would have to leave, the sooner the better.

She did not say so at once, but her closed face as she looked at her friend showed that troubled woman how futile were the early morning dreams. She got up at once, dressed and went out, refusing breakfast of any kind. Her appointment was not until the afternoon, but she felt safer moving about the streets, looking at shop windows, rather than waiting in Fothergill Mansions for the blow, the expected blow, to fall.

So she must go, she decided, but where? And how was she to find the means?

Archie would have to supply them. Was it not too soon? His performance the day before had been over-enthusiastic and markedly under-skilled. She had planned several days, even a whole week, of respite for him. Now it would have to be a rushed job, a crisis in her affairs, a rescue. With a threat behind it. For he had confessed the cause of his basic troubles as he lay with his head on her shoulder, recovering from his exertions. He would pay up all right, but he might still be a danger rather than an asset.

Not such a danger as Rosie. Now that the pigs knew it was Jim Bincott's body they had found, they would soon be directed back through his file to Rosie Lord and many others, including herself. So far, she told herself proudly, they had never been able to pin anything at all upon *her*. Nor, she prayed fervently, could they now. There had been suspicions over old Jaspar. Mrs Smith, damn her, would break like a rotten stick. Must have done by now. The young medicos, who had raised the first doubts, would still be unable to prove anything about Jaspar's death. She had been carried away, jerking him out of the wheelchair, but it was true he hadn't wanted to live. It really was suicide. So he had won, hadn't he? Curse him, all that followed was his fault, and the girl's, and Ma Smith's and now — Rosie.

Rosie was the weakest link in the chain, wasn't she? With Archie her own slave and Rosie out of the way, there could still be a future for her. There had to be. In nearly twenty years the Law had never caught up with her. She had no 'form' as the pigs called it.

Her terrified mind, circling incessantly around her past, her whole past, came back again and again to this conclusion. No form, no conviction.

They never would be able to pin anything on her, she boasted to herself, as she moved through the crowds, keeping close to the shop windows. They never would, they never would; she had out-smarted them all along the line. There wasn't a jury in the whole of Britain would feel it was 'safe', as she'd heard the judge say, to find her guilty and the bloody pigs knew it. The real safety was hers. It had to be.

Detective Chief Inspector Bartlet, however, felt he was approaching the point at which a murder charge in respect of the death of Jim Binscott was really getting nearer. At the time of the first renewal of the inquest on that well-known criminal, his identity and the details of his very nasty death had advanced the enquiry, but not far enough to reach a verdict. He had been on the run for a murder of his own. That was why he carried no wallet, no papers, no marks on his clothes. But he was Binscott and they had him at last.

The choice lay between accident and fiendishly contrived murder. But with no factual evidence to point to any likely individual responsible, which also meant capable of it, the coroner, while giving a certificate of the cause of death that would allow the corpse to be disposed of, did

147

not conclude the inquest, but adjourned it for a further period.

So Bartlet and Pearce were obliged to continue their search for Mrs Lawrence, who seemed to have vanished off the face of the earth. Or rather from the knowledge of all those who should have kept in touch with her. These, principally, were her solicitors in Carlisle, Mr Stone in Meadowfield, the unreliable Mrs Smith in Lincoln, the people at or near Hillside Farm and the local Social Services, represented by Mrs Chandler, who refused to discuss the matter on the grounds that as Mrs Lawrence had left Meadowfield she was no longer a client of hers, much as she had admired the long-suffering poor creature.

But this condition of utter frustration was broken one evening by the arrival at the police station of the reporter, Tine, with news of a discovery in Lawn Road, and a demand to see Detective Chief Inspector Bartlet right away.

Bartlet was in his room. The quickest way of getting rid of Tine, as the whole local force knew, was to listen to him. In five minutes Bartlet, Pearce and the reporter were on their way to The Old Farmhouse, where they found Mr Parsons, the neighbour with the dog of regular habits, who was standing just inside the gate, his pet sitting placidly beside him.

The find reported by Tine was still in the hedge, an untidy parcel, half covered by the earth the dog had scratched and kicked up over it. There was thick brown paper, torn blue knitting wool, and the handle, quite recognisable, of a medium-sized saw.

"My dog scratched and dug it out," Mr Parsons reported. "I haven't touched it. Mr Tine happened to be passing, and he got quite excited. I would have left it only I know Caesar would keep going back until I took it from him."

"You both did quite right," Bartlet said, producing a polythene bag to secure the whole find, paper, wool and instrument. "I'll ring your editor," he told Tine. He had become used to this young man's scoops, usually a nuisance, but sometimes, as now, a blessing.

He turned to the dog's owner.

"I must ask you, sir, to give me a statement of what exactly happened when Caesar dug this up. Was he off the lead, for instance, or were you both — er — trespassing?"

"Oh, for God's sake!" Mr Parsons burst out. "If I'd known the fuss about a simple — "

"Possible murder case," snapped the Chief Inspector. "Please, sir, I must ask very seriously for your co-operation."

"Oh, all right," Mr Parsons grumbled, only a little mollified by the policeman's respectful manner.

This was the origin of the paragraph in the daily paper that had bothered Rosie Lord and had driven Mrs Lawrence a long step nearer to fatal panic action.

When the police forensic laboratory had finished with the saw and its wrappings the cause of Binscott's death was perfectly clear. Mrs Lawrence had indeed laid a trap for her sometime lover and had murdered him. A country-wide search for her was now on.

Naturally the brief mention of fresh police evidence in the case of the criminal Binscott was enlarged and embellished in the account given by the local Meadowfield paper. It became a chief topic of conversation in the pubs and hotel bars. James Lawrence, who had missed it in the national press, soon heard it, variously told, in the lounge at The Sitting Duck. A new find. What could it be? Had they not sifted the contents of the cellar, indeed of the whole house and grounds?

Grounds! Why yes, of course. So the time had come to present his own contribution for what it might be worth.

He found Detective Chief Inspector Bartlet in his own room at the police station. He explained that he had come to enlarge upon his former statement about the evening of his arrival in Meadowfield.

"Oh," said Bartlet, "so you are the gentleman who was in the garden of The Old Farmhouse during the storm? I thought it might be you."

"You never asked me."

"I asked you for a detailed account of your movements that day. You chose to give me a shortened version. I should like to know why."

"Because I thought it would confuse you," said Lawrence blandly.

Bartlet swallowed his natural resentment, merely asking, "Why so, sir?"

"Because the whole development for me was such a complete surprise. I went to the house to meet my stepmother, who was quite unknown to me. There was a storm coming on — the father and mother of a storm. I saw a light on in the porch as I walked up the road, but I needed immediate shelter and found it in a small toolshed, unlocked, near the garage."

"Go on."

"When the rain eased off I saw a figure in a mac with a head scarf run out from the back of the house, dash across to the hedge near the gate, stoop, as I thought to look into the road and dash back. I slipped out myself, thinking I might now go up to the front door. But I was too late. Someone else, a man in an anorak with the hood up, was already just inside the gate."

"How did you know it was a man?"

"Big feet, long stride. Big hand on the gate. Obviously a man."

"Go on."

"As soon as he was inside the house the porch light went off."

"So what did you do then?"

"Well I thought it wouldn't do to have my first interview with Dorothy Lawrence when she had a visitor already. The rain had stopped. I had a look at the outside of the house. There was a light behind curtains in a front room

150

and a light through chinks in shutters at the back which I took to be the kitchen."

"You heard nothing?"

"No. I didn't go right up to the windows. I wasn't snooping, damn it, just taking a general look at the ancestral home. I didn't really want to meet my stepmother at all. She had nothing whatever to do with me or my life or my ancestors. The farm here did."

He spoke with feeling so that Bartlet was inclined to accept his statement as probably true. Besides, according to the landlord of the pub down the road, someone had seen a man in the garden during the lull in the storm. That fitted.

"Who did you think you saw run out to the hedge, or the gate, in the rain?"

"A woman, but it could have been a tallish boy. No, a woman really, by the way the scarf was tied over the head."

"You did not think it must be Mrs Lawrence?"

"No." James Lawrence was surprised. Odd he never did think it must have been Dorothy. "No," he repeated, "I suppose I took it for granted, as she appeared round the house from the back that it must be a servant."

"In this day and age?"

"We had two women who worked in the house at Hillside. My mother helped with the dairy and the hens while we ran the farm. She cooked, too."

There seemed to be no more to add. Mr Lawrence sat back, looking relaxed.

"Not much help, I'm afraid," he said, with a question in his voice.

"Everything helps," the Chief Inspector answered. "Even if it only clears the air."

"What does that mean?"

"It means I was right to conclude you had been up to The Old Farmhouse the day you got here. And now you have given me your account of the visit. I am glad to have it."

Both men stood up, moving slowly towards the door of the room. Mr Lawrence said goodbye, but made no apology for his delay in speaking out.

"I suppose," Bartlet asked, with a grim little twist of his mouth, "you wouldn't like to tell me where Mrs Lawrence may be found at the present time?"

"I haven't done away with her," Lawrence murmured in the same manner. "I'm leaving that to you chaps. And good luck to you."

But luck was as elusive as ever, so Detective Chief Inspector Bartlet thought he would have another go at Mrs Chandler. She had not acted her part of total ignorance very well, he felt. Surely with the amount of help and encouragement Mrs Lawrence had received from the Social Services it was most unlikely that her case would be dropped so entirely. Of course Mrs Chandler was anti-police like the majority of these do-gooders. But to insist she neither knew nor cared where Mrs Lawrence might be now? That did not ring true. That, he felt, was as false and as stupid as her basic attitude to law and order. The truth here was being smothered by sheer obstinacy. An obstinate woman who was also a fool was the bloody limit, Bartlet told Pearce as they drove off to visit the Social Services Office once more.

The junior staff there seemed very quiet and serious, but not over-awed by their arrival. Mrs Chandler was totally unchanged.

"I have already explained to you, officer," she said in her haughtiest manner, "that the unfortunate Mrs Lawrence, I should say, Mrs Wilson, is no longer on our books and I have no further information to give you about her or her case."

"You don't know where she is?"

"I do not."

"Nor which branch of the Social Services or which area she is probably applying to now? You advised her about Seacombe, didn't you?"

"When she decided to take Mr Lawrence there, yes."

"It was your advice that decided her to take the old gentleman away from here, wasn't it?"

"I advised a change of air, yes. She badly needed a holiday."

"And a change of scene and a change of medical attention?"

Mrs Chandler's rigid face for the first time softened and flushed.

"I felt she was not getting properly sympathetic treatment. That too needed a change."

The arrogant obstinacy was back. They were making no progress.

Detective Chief Inspector Bartlet said carefully, "It does seem that Mrs Lawrence relies on you a great deal, Mrs Chandler. Has she really made no attempt whatever, since she left Meadowfield, to get in touch with you? No appeal for help, even just for advice? No letter? No phone call? Really and truly nothing, Mrs Chandler?"

She remained silent, looking down at her desk, but she was remembering very clearly that recent call to the office: also that Beryl and Margery, who took the call in the first place, had both recognised the voice and commented upon it to one another and through Beryl to herself.

"There was one call," she said after a long pause. "It was made in the name of Wilson, her maiden name. She wanted me to know that she had reverted to it because her husband's will showed that he had left her nothing. All the property was to go to his son. She could no longer bear to use his name, she felt, poor woman."

"And that was all she had to say to you?"

"That was all."

Bartlet moved towards the door.

"You realise I need to confirm this call. It is most urgent for us to find Mrs Lawrence at once for her own sake as well as to complete the inquest on Binscott."

"What do you mean?" Mrs Chandler had also risen. He

must mean to question Beryl, perhaps Margery as well. "If you want to see my secretary I can call her in here," she went on, but Bartlet had gone, so she sank back into her chair, trying to remember at exactly what point in her whispered reply to Dorothy she had given her the ex-directory telephone number to her home.

Detective Chief Inspector Bartlet found Beryl in Mrs Chandler's reception area, made himself known to her and at the girl's own prompting, went downstairs to the telephone exchange where they gathered in Margery, leaving her place at the controls to one of the assistants.

He soon had the expanded story of Mrs Lawrence's call, together with the detail of her interview with Mrs Chandler. This included that whispered home telephone number that Beryl had taken down and locked away for future use if wanted.

"You would swear to this, each of you?" he asked the girls, "We may need signed statements, but Sergeant Pearce here has a verbal recording of our present conversation."

The girls stared at the junior detective, who stared back with a stony face, keeping his hands behind his back to avoid any involuntary fingering of his midget recorder.

"I remember the number, but you can have the paper I wrote it down on," Beryl said. "It's ex-directory."

"That's all right," Bartlet told her. "We can get it."

That and a good deal more, he decided, as he and Pearce left the building. From the Binscott end of the case they knew already a good deal about the man's association with a girl called Dorothy, or Dot Wilson, though she had never seemingly been mixed up with his criminal actions. And Dot, in her early days and his, had been a high-class call-girl, one of a group living in what was now called Greater Manchester, her particular friend there being known as Rosie Lord.

So perhaps now, with certain provisions made, they would be able to intercept any further calls from Mrs

154

Dorothy Lawrence or Wilson to her friend and protector Mrs Chandler. In the meantime they ought to be able to locate Rosie, if she was still in business and discover the actual whereabouts of the missing woman. For the evidence against her was mounting, though by no means complete.

"Not an open and shut case, sir, yet, is it?" asked Detective Sergeant Pearce.

"Too bloody open," answered Bartlet. "But it looks as if she may have gone to ground in her old haunts. We must have her in to question her and break her down. She killed Binscott for sure as far as I'm concerned. Now that we can guess where we're likely to find her we can certainly locate old Rosie Lord through the boys up there. That ought to flush out Dot, don't you think?"

"Should do, sir," Pearce said, the hunting instinct showing bright in his young eyes.

16

SHEER EXHAUSTION BROUGHT Mrs Lawrence's wanderings to an end. It was midday and she had neither eaten nor drunk since the evening of the day before. She found a bar that offered snacks, where a pork pie consisting mainly of crust and an ice ripple from the freezer helped down by a pint of stout, brought her back into fighting shape, if not to any real hope of success.

In this she was right. She kept her appointment with Mr Hill's department, but found herself unnoticed at the end of a line of other applicants. When her turn came at last she found herself facing Mrs Lone.

"Mr Hill is not here today," the fat secretary told her.

This was an unexpected setback, not to be borne.

"But I have an appointment," she insisted. "It is very urgent. Please tell him — "

"Mr Hill is not available," repeated Mrs Lone.

Mrs Lawrence lost her head.

"But I saw his car as I came in," she said, her voice growing shrill as anger overlaid caution. "He must be here — in the building. I must see him."

Mrs Lone pressed a button on her desk.

"I have told you he is not available," she said firmly. "I must ask you to leave immediately. There are others waiting. I have sent for assistance to remove you from this department."

"You have, have you?" cried Mrs Lawrence. The anger

had passed to all-consuming, cold fury. "Then you can damn well call it off or I'll shout out all I know about our Archie. How would you like that, you stupid old cow?"

Mrs Lone was not stupid; she knew now that Mrs Wilson, as she called herself, was dangerous. She also guessed what Archie had done and while she began to plan how to protect him she cancelled any immediate action. She pressed the button on her desk again and said "As you were. The difficult client has gone."

"But she hasn't, has she?" said Mrs Lawrence, laying down her bag again on the secretary's table. "So what are you going to do about it?"

"Sit down," said Mrs Lone. "He's in conference, which is why I told you he was not available. I'll see if I can get him."

"You needn't bother," Mrs Lawrence said. "You can give him a full account of our conversation, which I'm sure you'd settled to do anyhow. I'm leaving, see, Mrs Lone, but I need money. A lot of money. You know my circumstances, they're on my file. I've decided to go abroad."

She paused, wondering how much she could ask, how much, between them, they were worth. Because she could be sure Mrs Lone, who had fallen down on her job to keep him on the straight and narrow, would have to save her own job in saving his. So she did not state a plain sum but said, thoughtfully, "I suppose he took advantage of my faint to get my address. So he knew where I was staying and that's how he was able to call. I was too ill and weak to withstand him so — "

"Rubbish!" cried Mrs Lone, surprising herself by the vehemence of her remark. It also brought to a halt in the threshold of the room, Archie Hill, who was in the act of entering.

"What's this?" he demanded. "Mrs Lone, is that the way to speak to my clients?"

157

"It is, to this one," said Mrs Lone, red in the face and near to tears.

"It was my fault," Mrs Lawrence apologised, very gently. "I'm afraid I upset her because I did try to insist on seeing you personally. I'm sure you were busy — in conference, it's called, isn't it? So I'm entirely to blame."

"I'm quite sure you are not," Mr Hill said, looking at Mrs Lone with cold, hostile eyes. "Come through, Mrs Wilson."

They disappeared into his room together and Mrs Lone wept.

The situation was now more tricky than ever, Mrs Lawrence decided. She must handle it extremely delicately. With Mrs Lone a crude ultimatum, passed on, might have been successful. But now here was this fool Archie, already hardly able to keep his hands off her, cursing his old nanny Lone for rudeness to his darling Dorothy, wanting to know how soon he could come to her again.

"Not for a long, long time, my dear," she said in a very mournful voice. "I have to go abroad."

"Abroad? Why on earth?"

His astonishment was ludicrous. She sank into the usual chair beside his desk, edging forward so that she could rest her hands on it, within reach of his.

"Rosie can't let me have that room any more. I must go. There is no one in this country now. But I have old friends in Paris if I can get to them. But how can I? The fare — in these days — "

She let silence fall between them. At last she lifted her eyes to his. "I daren't ask. I couldn't hope — "

"You can! You can! Anything. Only tell me."

She began to raise the hand on his desk. He snatched it, pressed it down, covered it with both his own. She whispered, in a desperate voice, "That you would go, too? Take me with you? No! You have a home here, a wife — Of course you can't leave it all. I mustn't say it!"

But she had said it. His surprise, his fear, grew as

astonishment gave way to comprehension. His understanding in turn merged with longing to drive him into
total recklessness and reached a climax of consent she had
not imagined possible. Mrs Lawrence saw victory ahead.
Another gentle appeal, perhaps a kiss.

But, alas, it was too late. The enemy next door struck.
The buzzer on Mr Hill's desk brought Mrs Lone's voice,
saying loudly and briskly, "There are six more people to
see you before we close, Mr Hill."

The spell was broken. His face told her that. She had
been right in the first place. The proposition had been put
to him too soon. She got up at once, raging inwardly.

"Forget what I said, dear Archie," she whispered, bend-
ing over him as he stayed, frozen, despairing, in his chair.
"Forget me too. Goodbye. I shall be gone tomorrow.
Goodbye."

He reached up to pull her face down and kiss her, but
he did not move otherwise and looking back from the door
she saw that he had his head in his hands and his shoulders
were heaving.

So would he come with the lolly or wouldn't he, she
asked Rosie, when she got back to Fothergill Mansions.
Because it really was serious this time.

"How do I know?" her friend said, markedly unsym-
pathetic. "He's in a spot, really. Practically on probation,
as you might say. On account of him having these
impulses over clients. Why he has to get that way in the
office, God knows. As if there wasn't all the comfort in
the world, so to speak, waiting for him outside."

"Here, I suppose you mean?" Dot spoke coldly. If this
was the way Rosie meant to hint at her going she had no
need to regret what she must now set about doing.

"I thought I'd give him till tonight to show up again,"
she went on. "Then I'll be off in the morning, if he stumps
up what I said I'd need."

"I'm glad to hear it," Rosie told her. "I don't want to
push you, dear, but I must say I think you'd be better

159

away from here. Abroad? Have you got a passport and that?"

"What d'you think? Old Jaspar took me to Paris for our honeymoon. On his, that was. But I got it altered before I left Meadowfield."

"So you were thinking of leaving the country all along?"

"Jim had to leave."

"On the run, of course. He never did a clean job, did he? Always mucked them up, losing his temper. Would you really have gone with him, Dot?"

She did not answer. How could she when she had gone through so much to avoid that dangerous action. She pulled her thoughts back to the present and asked, "What does Archie have to spend his money on? How does he live?"

"He's not married, if that's what you mean?"

"I know that. He as good as told me. What do they pay them?"

"How do I know? More than the medicos in the hospitals, I expect. A lot more than they're worth."

"You're a great help, aren't you?" Dot shook herself. "I'll be off and pack. Can I use your phone?"

"Of course, dear. Put the money in the box afterwards."

The call was to Mrs Chandler, another cry for help, another tale of woe because her friend had turned against her, she must leave her present lodgings. Homeless, penniless, there was nowhere else in England. Her only hope was to find her way abroad, to some friends in Paris where Mr Lawrence had taken her on their honeymoon. But how could she find the fare?

"Tell me where you are," Mrs Chandler said, all her old feeling for this client restored by the piteous voice of this tragic, always uncomplaining, forever unfortunate woman. "Tell me your address and I will somehow manage to send you enough to cover your journey."

"Oh, bless you, bless you!" came the heartbroken answer.

But as Mrs Chandler reached for biro and paper to write on, the call ended abruptly. She waited but it was not renewed. There was nothing she could do.

For Mrs Lawrence the decision to end the call was not deliberate at that point, but would have been necessary in any case. For the front door bell had just rung and Rosie had sped jerkily past her to answer it. Such was her fear of unwanted visitors that she broke her appeal to Mrs Chandler and rushed to her room, locking the door after her. When Rosie came knocking she could barely find the strength to call out, "Who is it?"

"Rosie, you nit!"

She unlocked the door. Her friend pushed in past her, then turned, holding out a bulging envelope.

"From your beau, dear. Feels useful to me. He wouldn't come in."

While Dot turned away to open the envelope Rosie flung herself into the wicker chair near the bed and said, with envy in her voice, "I must say, you do have all the luck. How much?"

"Enough to get away from here, which is what you want."

"You needn't be sarky. I've never refused you a room, have I, now or in the old days?"

"I paid you always, didn't I?"

"And now?"

Mrs Lawrence threw a five-pound note at her friend, which fell a trifle short of the armchair. Reaching for it, Rosie slid off on top of the money and while Dorothy watched, with contemptuous understanding, Rosie giggled feebly, trying at the same time to right herself and recover the note from the floor beneath her. She managed both in due course and was not too confused to acknowledge the gift.

"Did you leave enough for the call?" she added, remembering she had answered the bell and that was why she had come to Dot's room.

161

"I reversed the charge," answered Mrs Lawrence, aware that she had only just thought of this answer.

"I expect you're lying," Rosie told her.

Mrs Lawrence had no wish to start a quarrel. Rosie was not a regular alcoholic, but she had these lapses and they usually began when she was worried or excited. It did not occur to her that she herself, with her urgent difficulties, her increasing problems, had been the most likely cause of this one. She only thought that it might be useful in the furthering of those plans she had already made.

"I'll pack my things now," she said, as she helped Rosie to reach the door. "I'll get a train south this evening, if you like. Now he's been," she added.

"The sooner the better," said Rosie, partly restored by the shame of her collapse.

"Silly bitch," said Dot gently.

This was too much for her soft-hearted friend, who laid her head on the other's shoulder and wept. In the end they staggered to Rosie's bedroom with arms entwined, where Rosie sank on to the bed and Dorothy found the bottle and glass she had been using and set them near her on the bed table.

When she had finished packing she visited Rosie's room again. She was ready to leave, in a dress and coat with a hat on and gloves that matched her handbag. In fact the outfit she had worn when she first visited Mr Hill's office.

Rosie was still on the bed, but sitting up now. Dorothy fetched herself a glass which she half filled from the bottle beside the bed, as well as filling up Rosie's to the top. They drank to their future success wherever they might be. They exchanged an affectionate kiss.

Then Mrs Lawrence was gone and Rosie, feeling very relieved and rather sleepy, emptied her glass and lay back again on her pillows.

In Meadowfield the call to Mrs Chandler's home was noted and its origin traced.

"As we thought," Bartlet said. "Rosie Lord's present establishment. Our Mrs Lawrence, Dorothy Wilson that was, must have gone to earth there. Hope she hasn't taken off again before the Super gets there."

For the search for Mrs Lawrence had now become a murder hunt and the case had therefore been passed up the police hierarchy to Detective Superintendent Dow who was now on his way to Greater Manchester with Detective Sergeant Pearce to join the local police in making the long deferred arrest.

For the time being nothing further was being done in Meadowfield, since the police did not trust Mrs Chandler not to inform her late client of the moves to find and secure her. So unless the suspect was off again they could expect to see her in the company of Detective Superintendent Dow, with luck inside twenty-four hours.

Having explained this twice to Sergeant Thomas, who was still working on patrol in Meadowfield, he went on to speculate.

"I'm telling you this, Thomas," he said, "because if our Mrs Lawrence is on the loose again, after making this call to Mrs Chandler, which she very well may be, I think the odds are strongly in favour of her turning up again in this town."

"Surely not," Sergeant Thomas protested. "Why on earth?"

"The usual, of course. Money. God knows what she's been living on since she scarpered the night she did in Jim Binscott. But she managed to squeeze the Social Services here, so she may have done the same up there. I know Detective Superintendent Dow asked his opposite number to have a look at them."

"She'd be mad to come back, sir, wouldn't she?"

"They often are." Bartlet, who was feeling ill-used because the case in its last stages had been taken from him, found solace in displaying wisdom to the young.

"They get reckless. They think they're immune; nothing can touch them. Emotional. Megalomaniacs."

"Cold-blooded, I'd say," protested Sergeant Thomas.

Detective Chief Inspector Bartlet let this pass. He was not going to argue.

"Well," he said. "Just keep your eyes open for anyone like this bitch, Lawrence. The sooner she's put away the better. I don't say she *will* turn up in Meadowfield. I say she might."

"If we don't hear by tomorrow that she's been found and charged."

"She'll be charged here, if Dow finds her."

But she was not found. Detective Superintendent Dow made himself known at the local police station serving Fothergill Mansions late that night. They had checked earlier that evening that a Mrs Wilson was staying at Number Three and was attending the Social Services branch under Mr Archibald Hill, whose secretary a Mrs Lone, confirmed her interviews with him.

Mr Hill, himself, appealed to later, at his own flat, confirmed that Mrs Wilson, who was also known as Mrs Lawrence, was living at Three, Fothergill Mansions. Detective Superintendent Dow decided to make his arrest that night. He did not want to miss his chance, even though the unavoidable noise of the event would upset the neighbours.

There was no noise, no upset, only the quiet arrival and a measure of delay before one of the young ladies of the house came down to open the door.

For Mrs Lawrence was by this time far away. Besides, Rosie Lord was no longer available for questioning. She was in her bed, lying peacefully under a blanket and quilt, fully dressed and dead.

17

IT WAS MISS CARR who recognised Mrs Lawrence in one of the main streets of Meadowfield, three days after the discovery of Rosie's death.

Miss Carr was pursuing her usual unproductive activities in and about the town. Mrs Chandler had not been able to have her moved to another district. Her useless handling of the case of Mr Lawrence had made very little impression upon the higher levels of administration. At these levels the weight of authority, as heavy as the salaries that went with the posts, was seldom brought to bear upon workers as lowly as Miss Carr, unless their mistakes or their deficiencies brought them into the never-ending series of reports that public outcry made necessary. Even so the reports, accepted as an obligation, hardly ever bore sanctions. The higher levels of administration preferred peace at all costs. Having climbed to the point where the active performance of good deeds was carried out by others and even the reports and accounts connected with it were got together by others, still climbing, the top levels preferred a quiet, comfortable period of consolidation before achieving the real summit, the acquisition of medal, title, even national acclaim.

Besides, Mr Lawrence's death at Seacombe removed his case from the books of Meadowfield and the resort. Without his record Mrs Chandler was helpless. Miss Carr's connection with the case was no longer relevant to her work, since it had become past history. Also there was no further need for speech therapy at present. So Miss Carr could continue to exercise her faulty methods and sadly lacking command of real modern psychology, upon a number of confused, dispirited persons on Mrs Chandler's list. In the course of which activity she suddenly caught sight of Mrs Lawrence, crossing a pedestrian precinct in the centre of Meadowfield.

Her first feeling was of pleasure, the pleasure of recognition, of meeting an absent friend after a long interval. Her first impulse was to hurry after Mrs Lawrence, catch her up, welcome her, ask her if she was back at The Old Farmhouse.

The Old Farmhouse? Even Miss Carr remembered in time the wholly sinister events connected with the place where she had enjoyed such pleasant conversations and accepted such willing hospitality from the woman who was still passing, but further away now, on the other side of the precinct.

Besides, though she had recognised her former client and friend, surely she must be far from well. There had been something different in her walk, less brisk, and her face, thinner, wasn't it, though you didn't see faces very clearly with the modern felt hat pulled down over the eyes, like her own grandmother had worn in those old photos of the twenties.

So, in the end, Miss Carr followed her usual habit of taking no definite action. But she did mention the fact of seeing Mrs Lawrence when she went back to the office at the end of the day. It was Beryl she spoke to, who saw more importance in Miss Carr's casual bit of gossip than the psychiatric social worker had done.

"I think you should tell Mrs Chandler," Beryl said. If it was true, the police ought to know, but that would come better from the boss than from herself. She wanted no part in what to was to follow, but she would warn Margery as well.

Mrs Chandler tried to conceal her shocked surprise. This was not difficult, because Miss Carr was not a noticing person and besides, being rather frightened of Mrs Chandler, she was thinking more about how to convey her news than upon its effect on Mrs Lawrence's constant supporter.

So the interview was soon over and Mrs Chandler hurried home that day in a very agitated state. She was thankful to find the bungalow dark, unoccupied.

But very cold. She turned on the central heating and boosted it in her sitting room with two lines of electric fire. She was too much upset to think about cooking herself her usual light supper to go with the programme on telly.

Why had Dorothy come back? Where had she been since the last time she had telephoned? Had she any connection with that short paragraph in the paper yesterday, or was it the day before, about a Miss Lord who had been found dead of a drug overdose. Possible suicide, the paper had it, or accident, because there was alcohol as well.

Mrs Chandler shivered even as she held out her hands to the electric fire. Why did she feel such dread on hearing that perhaps Dorothy was back in Meadowfield? Surely she did believe in her still, even after what those detectives had hinted about her? They were going to find her soon, because they had forced her to acknowledge that Dorothy had made contact by telephone. They could trace calls; she knew that. So if they found her, why was there nothing about her in the paper? Only this death. But why did she suspect that had anything to do with Dorothy?

She knew the answer that she was struggling to refute. Because the name in the paper was Rose Lord and Dorothy had said the last time she phoned that her friend's name was Rosie. Suicide or accident. So it had been with Mr Lawrence. Perhaps also with the man Binscott. Perhaps

Miss Carr was mistaken and it had not even been Dorothy. Pray God Miss Carr was mistaken.

But for once Miss Carr had made no mistake. Mrs Lawrence arrived a little after nine, exhausted to the point of speechlessness, haggard, trembling.

"Dorothy!" Mrs Chandler's ready compassion overlaid all her recent doubts and fears. "You look terrible! What have you been doing with yourself? Why didn't you — "

But Mrs Lawrence, without answering, pushed past her into the sitting room and sinking into the armchair Mrs Chandler had just left, crouched towards the fire, holding out her shaking hands towards it.

Mrs Chandler, following said, "You look all in! I don't keep spirits, but — "

Getting no response at all she went to her meagre shelf of bottles to pour the visitor a glass of sweet sherry. Mrs Lawrence took it without thanks and sipped it slowly, while her hands steadied and a little colour came back into her thin cheeks. At last she said, "I've been walking all day," and stared at Mrs Chandler as if that explained everything.

"When did you last eat?" the latter asked, still trying to restore the Dorothy she had known and liked.

"I don't remember."

"Then that's the next thing. Sit still. I'll get you something."

Mrs Chandler hurried away to prepare the light meal she had intended for herself. Anything she felt, to keep herself occupied until her guest recovered enough to explain herself. That she had come, as usual, for help she took for granted. Well, that was her job in life and she would continue to provide all she was able to hand out in the way of advice and encouragement as soon as she knew what the immediate problem was. From knowing she shrank with all her new found doubts, but a little later, watching Dorothy eat wolfishly the scrambled eggs and mushrooms and toast and drink two cups of black coffee, her curiosity revived in time with the visitor's marked recovery.

"I had to come south," Mrs Lawrence said at last, speaking almost in her old, incisive way. "I couldn't very well stay up there. The Social Services were not particularly helpful. At least your Mr Hill would have liked to be, but his secretary was a bit of a bitch. My friend — "

She paused, looking at Mrs Chandler to see what her reaction might be, before continuing the story she meant to tell.

"Your friend was this Miss Lord, wasn't it?" Mrs Chandler cried, not able to prevent herself interrupting the calm, even flow of Mrs Lawrence's explanation.

"Yes. Poor Rosie. She drank, I'm afraid."

"You know this?"

"For years. There were times when she pulled herself together. But she never held out for long. They don't, do they?"

"That depends." Mrs Lawrence was prepared to defend her own list of alcoholics against this sweeping statement. "But go on. Was she so desperate about herself that she turned to suicide to end it?"

Mrs Lawrence appeared to consider. "I think it may have been that," she said at last. "Poor Rosie. She was always bright and cheerful to strangers. Even to me, though I knew so much about her. But you see she knew quite well it was dangerous to mix her drinks. Drugs and alcohol and all that. Taking all the sleeping pills in the bottle on top of her usual. That was enough to knock out a horse."

"Do they know that?" asked Mrs Chandler, quite innocently. "I didn't think they'd held the inquest yet? Was there a police report? I only saw the one short — "

Mrs Lawrence's face was changing alarmingly. It grew red with anger, her eyes glared, her mouth opened in a snarl of rage.

"Inquest! Police!" she shouted in a voice Mrs Chandler had never heard before. "What have they to do with it?

169

Or with me? Don't you believe what I'm telling you, you bloody smug bitch?"

Shocked to the very core of her being by this outburst, Mrs Chandler could only protest, trying feebly to argue that she did not mean to upset Dorothy. But the only thing she found to say was by no means soothing, quite the opposite.

"Dorothy, please! I am here to help you, not to attack you. But you must understand that your evidence about those pills will have to be produced to the coroner. It suggests suicide, as you say, not accident."

"I'd left," Mrs Lawrence panted, trying to control her temper. "I don't know a thing. They can't question me. No one can. I'd gone."

"Very well. But it isn't only that. You must know the police want to talk to you, have done so ever since you went back to Hillside."

She dared not refer to that other, twice adjourned, inquest on the criminal in the cellar.

"They only want your address, Dorothy. So why not give it to them? You didn't give it, even to me, did you?"

"So you couldn't give it for me, could you? Have they asked for it?"

"Of course they have." Mrs Chandler felt she was beginning to get the situation under control again, but this made her blunder once more.

"I told them you were off our books, as you still are, but I didn't tell them I had recommended Archie Hill."

"A fat lot of good he was, too."

"I was forced to acknowledge you had rung me up."

"You did *what*?"

The rage was growing again, her hands clenching, the eyes glaring. Mrs Chandler tried to fight down her own response of sickening fear.

"I had to agree that I had spoken to you because Beryl took the call, I mean Margery. And Beryl too, of course."

"Your two zombies, yes, of course, damn you to hell!"

"My number here is ex-directory. Neither of them — "

"Be your age! Grass and grass again! Like old Smith, the bloody cow in Lincoln!"

Mrs Lawrence was out of her chair now, walking about the room with violent strides, knocking against the furniture, sweeping ornaments to the floor, tearing the flex from the television set, seizing the telephone receiver for similar treatment.

But she changed her mind, when she saw that Mrs Chandler, watching her, had her attention chiefly riveted upon the telephone. This second outburst was replaced, like the first, by her usual calm; icy, clear, pitiless.

She put down the receiver again on the table where the rest of the apparatus, with a notebook beside it, stood waiting for calls. The disconnected machine lay buzzing faintly. Then she went to stand in front of Mrs Chandler, who still cowered in her chair near the fire.

"I'm going abroad," she said. "You've got to help me."

"I can't," Mrs Chandler told her. "Dorothy, how can I?"

Dorothy struck her across the face.

"How? The wherewithal, of course, you fool! Notes. Travellers' cheques. Don't tell me you're not good for five hundred."

"Five hundred pounds? Impossible!"

Mrs Lawrence went away into the kitchen and came back with what Mrs Chandler recognised as her only really sharp kitchen knife.

"We won't talk about impossibles," Dorothy said, in such a deadly tone that her miserable benefactor shrank so far into her chair that the back of it creaked like a storm-bent mast.

"I'm staying here tonight. I thought you'd come up with the needful willingly. I can see the pigs have got at you. Well, that's out. So you'll slip me a note and a cheque to cash to bearer and we'll have to forget about the travel-

171

lers' cheques. I'll be away to get to the bank before it opens."

"They won't cash it. There isn't enough in my account to cover it."

"Oh, is that how it is?" So even her Social Service ladyship was not above diddling the inland revenue. "Where is it, then? How much?"

With the knife at her throat, Mrs Chandler, sobbing and gasping, revealed her nest-egg, her tax-free, non-dividend-bearing small savings and bonuses of the last fifteen years. Mrs Lawrence counted it out, found it more than sufficient for her immediate needs, and restored the empty box to its hiding place.

When Mrs Chandler gasped, "You are a wicked, deceitful woman! I could not have believed — !" Mrs Lawrence laughed gaily in her triumph, prepared to go on her way to final escape immediately.

But Mrs Chandler was driven to the courage of despair. She got up, brushing her self-exposed enemy out of her way and dashed for the door, meaning to run and shout for help before Dorothy could catch her.

She got out of her sitting room and halfway along her short hall before her attacker caught up with her and sent her headlong with a well-placed foot. She twisted her ankle as she fell, so that when she managed to raise herself she found she could do no more than hobble back to the chair she had left.

"Serve you right," said Dorothy in her coldest voice. "You'll go to bed now."

"I can't walk. I've twisted my ankle."

It was true. Unaided, Mrs Chandler found it impossible to put any weight on the injured leg. Dorothy had to help her to get undressed and finally to crawl into the bed with a folded scarf bound round the ankle, now swollen to twice its proper size.

While they were doing this Mrs Lawrence noticed that there was another telephone on the small bedside table.

"Extension?" she asked.

"Yes, of course."

In the act of putting this one too out of action, Dorothy paused. Was it wise to isolate the house? If what Violet had told her about the police was true, they would be suspicious at once if they tried to get in touch with her and found they couldn't do so. Therefore leave the receivers on; this one she could put out of reach by moving the table away from the bed. The other one, restored, was already out of reach. She could guard it herself for the rest of the night. In the morning she would be away. Safer perhaps to go at once? No. The mood of recklessness that had followed her first success with Archie came upon her again, so she stayed.

She was rewarded, she found. Half an hour later the phone rang. She took the receiver to Violet, standing beside her, again with the knife in her hand, to direct the answers. A man was asking a question.

"Is that Inspector Bartlet?" Mrs Chandler asked, looking up sideways at Dorothy. "No? Then who is it?"

She repeated the answer, "Detective Superintendent Dow? I don't think I know you."

Her voice was shaky, going up and down unevenly, with a deep breath between words that came with difficulty from her dry throat and lips.

"No," she answered the next question and repeated it so that Dorothy would understand. "No, I haven't seen Mrs Wilson at the office today. No, nor here either."

There was a further short speech from the other end, to which Mrs Chandler replied, "I can't help it if I sound agitated. I am agitated. I have just fallen in my hall — my bungalow — and hurt my ankle. No, not broken, I hope, but very painful. I'm in bed."

Again a pause for the superintendent to speak.

"If it's still painful in the morning, I shall ring the office. No, I'm sure I don't need a doctor. Is that all? I am tired and I've taken aspirin and I want to try to sleep. It's very late."

She broke off the call and Mrs Lawrence at once moved the bed table out of reach again. Neither of them spoke. There was nothing to say and nothing to do until the morning.

But the police had quite a different picture of the course of events in Meadowfield that day, or rather that afternoon and evening. Though Miss Carr had gone only to Mrs Chandler with her news, Tine in his usual search for interesting events and gossip, had also recognised a face he could identify. But without real certainty, from several newspaper photographs only. Changed a good deal, too, looking far from well, but then the woman was on the run, wasn't she, and must know it.

He took his doubtful information to Detective Superintendent Dow, whom he knew was now in charge of the search for the missing woman.

Dow, who was getting browned off by the total lack of success of any of his lines of enquiry, was ready to snatch at any news, however feebly supported. But he was not going to let young Tine know this. He thanked the reporter, told him he would be in touch with his editor about any developments and as soon as the young man had left the station called in Detective Chief Inspector Bartlet to help in the much-needed arrest. They had been prepared for it and if Tine was right Bartlet's hunch was working out.

"No one left for her to appeal to except Mrs Chandler," the detective repeated. "I fully believe that's where she'll go for the night. Probably there now. What are we waiting for?"

"Confirmation. Tine himself wasn't sure. He's never actually seen her. It occurs to me we might ask round the patrol cars, warn them to look out for her, but not to do anything to frighten her, such as following or ques-

174

tioning. She's dangerous. Would you agree to that?"

"Of course," answered Bartlet, knowing that the word would go forth whether he agreed or not.

Before darkness fell Sergeant Thomas with Constable Hill had picked up the trail. They had not of course seen Mrs Lawrence at the time of the discovery of Jim Binscott's body, but that episode had been a highlight in their young careers and they had made themselves familiar with all the available photographs. So when, on a pedestrian crossing, a thin woman in a floppy hat shading a haggard face raised an imperious hand to stop them, Constable Hill exclaimed, almost before she was out of hearing, "That's our bird, the murderess! Get it through to Dow, sarge!"

"Detective Superintendent Dow to you, constable."

This confirmed Tine. At the police station the senior detectives laid their plans for the arrest. But first of all Dow decided to ring up Mrs Chandler; the result was disturbing.

"Mrs Chandler says she's sprained her ankle. May be true. She's in a proper tizz over it, but I think our villain's there all right."

"Question is," said Bartlet solemnly, "if her injury was a real accident or Mrs L attacked her. She's quite capable of it with her history, especially this case, and her background."

"You mean it'd be safer to put a guard on and take Lawrence when she leaves the bungalow in the morning, rather than making an entry tonight."

"That's what I have in mind."

"We could use this injury though, to get in, couldn't we?"

So all the arrangements were made and the wanted woman was considered sufficiently dangerous for Dow to provide himself and Bartlet with firearms in case of need.

Before they broke up their meeting Dow said, "Mrs

Chandler seemed to think she'd be going in to work tomorrow morning as usual. Refused to see a doctor tonight. Will you explain this to Dr Harris. We're relying on him getting into the house before we do and without putting the wind up our villain. We can follow at once."

"By the back garden?"

"Either side. But Dr Harris must be warned what to expect."

So Bartlet rang up Geoff Harris to inform and prepare him. Together they arranged to call an ambulance and to notify the Social Services at the same time.

Naturally Geoff rang up Lucy and she, considering that Mr Lawrence was being both kind and patient, rang up The Sitting Duck with her news. This made him thank her for whetting his appetite for further excitement. He said he would sit by his phone in the morning until she discovered what actually had happened to Mrs Chandler.

But after she rang off he made another couple of calls to satisfy his curiosity and later, when he went to bed, he asked reception to have him called the next morning at seven promptly.

18

MRS CHANDLER SPENT a wretched night, dozing from time to time when exhaustion defeated fear, then, as a stab of pain in her ankle followed an attempt to turn over, waking to a fresh misery of doubt and terror.

Dorothy did not come near her all night, nor did she make any noise elsewhere in the bungalow. She might be gone, Mrs Chandler thought, hoping against common sense that it was so. Not to be expected during those hours when solitary travellers were more likely than at any time in the twenty-four, to be noticed by sleepless citizens at their bedroom windows or by policemen on foot or in their patrol cars. No. Dorothy would go when she said she would, when she could very quickly mingle with all the early throng going to work, to their shops or factories, to their commuter trains.

When at least the long night did come to an end Mrs Lawrence walked into Mrs Chandler's room, pulled back the curtains, showing a pale early morning sky and asked in a calm, cool voice, "Well, how's the leg?"

"I can't use it," Mrs Chandler told her. "I tried an hour ago. I had to — the toilet — "

She lay flat, looking up at her tormentor with piteous eyes.

"Use a jerry, do you?" Dorothy said, stooping to look under the bed. "Manage all right?"

"No. If it was on a chair — "

With a chair drawn up to the bed and Dorothy holding the jerry on it with one hand and with the other supporting Mrs Chandler, her injured hostess and benefactress was suitably relieved. When the whole performance was over and Mrs Chandler was back in bed, sitting up against pillows, Dorothy said, "I'm going to make myself a cuppa before I go. Like one?"

"Oh yes, please," Mrs Chandler roused herself further. "I can't go to work. That's obvious, isn't it? I ought to ring Beryl and tell her — "

"What will you tell her?"

The cold, savage look was back; Mrs Chandler shivered.

"Why, that I've fallen and sprained my ankle, of course. That I'll be off duty for a few days."

She looked away, biting her lips, remembering the routine that she held with such severity over any illness among her staff. "I'll have to see a doctor. For a certificate. Always insist."

"That copper was on to you last night. He asked if you'd had a doctor."

"I said I didn't need one."

"Now you say you do. Not till I've gone. Understand?"

"I've got to phone. I must phone Beryl, mustn't I?"

Unwillingly Dorothy brought the bed-table back from the corner where she had put it the night before. She watched Mrs Chandler dial the Social Services office, address the night caretaker, ask for Margery, who was not in yet, leave a message for Beryl and ring off, not giving her home address or phone number.

"How will Beryl know where to ring you?" Dorothy asked, suspiciously. "I thought you said this was ex-directory?"

"In case of illness or emergency, she can get it from headquarters," Mrs Chandler told her, not revealing that she knew her secretary had it already as well as the address of the bungalow.

"What time does Beryl get in?"

"Nine sharp."

"Sharp, is it?" Dorothy mocked. "Well, I'm off at half-eight, sharp, see."

"The kettle's boiling," said Mrs Chandler, who had heard it begin to whistle before she finished her call.

"Damn the kettle!" said Dorothy, lifting the telephone out of Mrs Chandler's reach before she left the room, leaving the door open behind her.

The kitchen lay opposite Mrs Chandler's bedroom and its window looked out on the side of the bungalow, with the back door set in the same wall. Directly after Mrs Lawrence had snatched up the kettle to pour boiling water on to a tea-bag already suspended in a china tea-pot, she heard a knock at the back door. A pause, and the knock was repeated.

"Who is it?" she called, still pouring. It must be a tradesman, she decided, hopefully the milk, for there was none in the fridge and no tins or powder in the cupboard.

"Milk," a man's voice called back.

"Coming!"

He must want his money, she thought. What a time to call. Tell him to leave it? Risky. The more she said the more he was likely to find her voice a stranger's, not his customer.

The tea-pot was full. She put the kettle on the stove, pulled back two bolts on the door and opened it.

A tall man stood outside, holding a bottle of milk, which he thrust forward into her hands. As she moved back with it, saying politely, "Thank you", he followed her in, turning at once, not to go out again, but to shut the door and stand with his back to it.

Dorothy put down the milk bottle on the table. She stared at the stranger, her face whitening, but she said nothing. It must be the Law. Let him declare himself first.

"You are very silent, Dorothy," the invader said. "I am

James Lawrence, your late husband's son. You are my stepmother."

"The hell I am!" she burst out furiously.

"You are, indeed," he went on. "Pour me out a cup, too, Dorothy. I have quite a lot to say to you."

It was then they heard Mrs Chandler's quavering voice calling from the bedroom, "He's right, Dorothy. He *is* Mr James Lawrence. He *is* your stepson. I know him."

"You see," said Mr Lawrence, taking the tea-pot and pouring the tea, because Dorothy seemed to be paralysed, standing rigidly behind the table, staring and staring at the large cheerful man who in build and strong, determined face reminded her, with a sickening screw of fear in her chest and throat, of the man she had planned to exploit and finally to destroy.

Mr Lawrence loaded three cups of tea on to a small tray and carried it into Mrs Chandler's bedroom. Dorothy followed, outwardly subdued, indeed hardly aware of what she was doing, while her mind darted here and there, trapped in her consternation at this totally unexpected development, this new, most terrible obstacle to her escape.

"I am sorry to see you are ill, Mrs Chandler," he said, handing her a cup from the tray, which he had put down on the top of a chest of drawers. "Your bed-side table," he went on, "you'll need that and your telephone, won't you?"

Glancing at Mrs Lawrence he added, "I suppose that was your doing, Dorothy, moving it out of her reach. For really nasty tricks you do take the biscuit, don't you?"

As she made no answer, but continued to sip her tea, half turned away from the bed, Mrs Chandler defended her.

"You must not abuse visitors in my house, Mr Lawrence. Dorothy is terribly overwrought, on the verge of a breakdown. She needs — "

"A very big dose of the truth," interrupted Lawrence. "Acknowledged by herself, understood by you, who persist, which I can hardly believe, in ignoring the plain facts of her behaviour, which has been evil throughout this whole business. Evil, wicked, or is that a dirty word in this benighted country? Perhaps only in your fatuous section of it. Your Dorothy is a multiple murderess. She tried to starve my father to death and when that was frustrated she drowned him."

"Liar!" Dorothy screamed. "All lies!"

Though her guilt was plain now in her distorted face, Mrs Chandler still fought for her, or perhaps chiefly for her own pride, her own vanity.

"Surely she had no motive to do such a terrible thing?" she persisted.

"She had motive all right. She knew, or she thought she knew, that he had left her The Old Farmhouse. Jim, the criminal, egged her on to get rid of him and cash in on the property. His stroke played into their hands. He was made defenceless."

"You did nothing to help him, did you?" said Mrs Chandler, still fighting, though more feebly.

"I was not told of it until after his death. She never wrote to me, not a single letter from first to last."

"I didn't have your address," Mrs Lawrence said, speaking clearly for the first time since they had joined Mrs Chandler.

"Rubbish!" He turned on her. "You fool! You, all-time God-damned idiot! Did it never occur to you that *I* might help you? Sympathise even? A young woman landed with an old invalid husband and her legacy denied her because she'd run off the rails with a much younger man? A rather ordinary tale these days. I'm not a Victorian prude, Dorothy. If you'd been a normal woman I would probably have been ready to set you up. But you're not normal. You're rotten all through. Cunning, but stupid too, only your vanity will never let you see that."

The front door bell, a jingle of notes, rang clearly in the silence that followed his outburst. As neither of the women

181

spoke or moved, Mr Lawrence said sharply, "That'll be the doctor. Let him in, Dorothy."

There was no response, so he moved towards her, seized her from behind by her shoulders and propelled her out of the room and across the hall, saying, quite quietly, "All right. We'll let them in together."

The action was so swift, the hands on her shoulders so strong that Mrs Lawrence found herself obeying and moving without power, mental or physical, to resist. At the door, as they stopped, she tried to break free, but Mr Lawrence merely said, "Open it, Dorothy!"

Furious and humiliated, she obeyed again, to meet the smiling faces of Geoff and Lucy.

She felt her stepson's hands drop from her shoulders, but even this relief did nothing at all to restore her.

"You!" she gasped. "*Both* of you!" She addressed herself chiefly to Geoff. "Surely you aren't Mrs Chandler's doctor? Who sent you? Was it Beryl?"

"We had a call to the Group surgery," explained Geoff. "A message about a fall and a twisted ankle. That's why I thought Lucy might be useful."

"But — but — " Frantically searching for a believable cause to account for this intrusion, frantically driving away the only real meaning it could have, Dorothy Lawrence pulled the door wider open, let the newcomers pass her, then stammered, "But it isn't nine o'clock yet. It can't have been Beryl. Mrs Chandler is in bed, still. We haven't had breakfast. We aren't prepared."

"The message was an urgent one," Geoff told her. "So naturally as the new boy in our Group it came to me. Which is Mrs Chandler's room?"

Still dazed, but beginning at least to plan a different form for her escape, she said, with a sidelong glance of hatred at Mr Lawrence, "He knows the room. He'll show you." Then she disappeared quickly into the other room she had occupied the night before and the three heard the key turn in the lock.

Mrs Chandler submitted to Geoff's examination of her ankle with quiet resignation. His gentle handling and his thoroughness impressed her against her will and at the end of it she was willing to accept his advice.

"I hope it is no more than a bad sprain," he told her, "but we must have an X-ray. Anyway you can't stay here by yourself, as you are. May I use your phone? We'll have an ambulance to take you up to the hospital. I'll stay to see you aboard. But Lucy and Mr Lawrence ought to go home now, I think."

"So do I," said Mr Lawrence, going up to the bed to take his leave and make his apologies for invading her bungalow without being invited.

In the passage outside, Mrs Lawrence, wearing the now shabby coat and felt hat in which she had arrived and with her handbag slung over her arm, paused beside a cupboard door where she had found cleaning utensils the night before. It also had a shelf on which were a pair of secateurs, a small plastic container of rooting powder and a packet of a strong chemical weed-killer. She took this last and continued on her way to the kitchen.

They would need breakfast, she thought, with luck all five of them. Her enemies, her betrayers, her delayers. So she would put out the things they would need and then go. If the powder she had in her hand got mixed into the instant coffee and they didn't notice it, that wasn't her fault, was it?

She lifted the big coffee-jug from the back of the stove to the kitchen table, with the weed killer packet still in her hand. She stooped to the kitchen drawer for a spoon. A voice from beside the tall kitchen cupboard said, "Put down that packet, Mrs Lawrence and stand away from the table."

Jerking upright she saw a grey-haired, stocky individual in a neat dark suit. He had been hidden when she came in by the side of the cupboard. He moved a hand to show her his badge.

"Detective Superintendent Dow," he said. "You are Dorothy Lawrence, I think."

She did drop the packet of weed-killer, but she could not obey the order to move for she was paralysed by astonishment and fear. Instead she caught at the table to stop herself from falling. When at last she managed to speak it was only to say in a whisper, "How did you get in?"

"The back door was open," Dow told her. "You opened it to Mr James Lawrence, your stepson."

Instantly she saw a gleam of hope.

"He pretended to be the milkman. He forced his way in. I had never seen him before, never in my life. He must have known his way to the bungalow. He — "

"Mr Lawrence has been in Meadowfield for some time. He came from Canada to clear up his father's affairs. Has he not told you that?"

"Yes, he has. And more besides. Threats! Accuses me — "

She swayed where she stood.

"Where is he now?" Dow asked, going to her side, but making no move to help her.

"With Mrs Chandler and the doctor and that girl they call Lucy."

Dow nodded.

"You sent them!" she accused him. "You sent them all, didn't you?"

"Not Mr Lawrence. Nor Miss Summers. So you left them all with Mrs Chandler, did you, while you made them coffee, yes? Laced, perhaps with the contents of this?"

He produced a polythene bag from his pocket and carefully slid the packet into it. "A leaving present for all of them, was it to be, Mrs Lawrence. A poison without an antidote. You knew that, did you? Of course you did. You were intending to go away, right away, this time, weren't you?"

"I am going abroad," she said, recovering her usual

calm voice. "But first you must arrest James Lawrence."

"Arrest Lawrence? What for?"

He tried not to show surprise, nor the sneaking admiration he could not but feel for her quick cunning, her grasp of the one doubt the police still held regarding Lawrence's behaviour on the night of the storm.

"For the murder of Jim Binscott," she said, answering his question.

"Take me to him," Dow ordered.

In Mrs Chandler's room Geoff at once reported his provisional diagnosis of Mrs Chandler's injury and explained why he had brought Lucy with him and that he had ordered an ambulance which should arrive at any minute now. Mr Lawrence apologised for jumping the gun, and explained that Geoff had told him the form for this morning, but he decided a little extra help might be needed to get the doctor admitted and to protect Mrs Chandler until the police arrived.

Detective Superintendent Dow was not very pleased to hear this bald revelation of his careful plans, for it caused Mrs Lawrence to cry, "A put-up job from start to finish, was it? I thought as much!" She followed this with an immediate verbal attack on her stepson, finishing with a demand for his immediate arrest.

James Lawrence was not disturbed. Before the superintendent could make any answer he repeated the statement he had made to Detective Chief Inspector Bartlet. Mrs Lawrence persisted.

"You were hiding in the garden," she panted. "I might have known it. You waited till I'd gone, then you broke in. You forced Jim into the cellar. You killed him. Murderer!"

Dow said, "Mr Lawrence was back in his hotel by nine. We have checked, of course. You were seen in Lawn Road, leaving in the early hours next morning. Whether he saw you getting rid of a parcel or not, a dog found the parcel in the hedge. The saw inside carries your fingerprints and there are fragments of the blue wool on the

185

ladder as well as in the parcel. This charge of yours doesn't begin to stand up, Mrs Lawrence. On the other hand it must have been you who turned out the lights in the house when you left, for they *were* put out, *after* Binscott fell."

"His body accuses you, Dorothy," James Lawrence told her. "He didn't die quickly. He tried to crawl to where he knew the ladder must have been, because he saw the line of light under the cellar door. Was he shouting for help, screaming in pain, while you packed your bundle and stole his anorak? Was he still calling to you when you turned out the hall light and locked the cellar door and left the poor devil to die in the dark?"

She stood rigid, cold-eyed as ever, totally unmoved by the picture he drew. Mrs Chandler hid her face in her hands; Lucy looked white and sick.

"I'm sorry, my dear," Mr Lawrence said to her, taking her arm. "Perhaps we may go now?" he asked Dow, who nodded agreement.

"Yes, you go, Lucy. I'm going to see Mrs Chandler on to the ambulance." Geoff repeated his intention, not asking permission from anyone, least of all the patient.

As the two left Detective Chief Inspector Bartlet and Sergeant Pearce came in through the front door and passed them, going towards the room they had just left.

"What happens now?" Lucy asked, shakily.

"Probably, if she agrees, they'll take her away to the police station to charge her and make the arrest."

They moved across the small lawn towards the road.

"I came in Geoff's car," she said as they reached the edge of the road.

"I'll take you back in mine. It's up the road. A bit boxed in by the Force now, I see."

There were, indeed, several police cars ranged along the kerb but with a wide space left opposite the path from the bungalow. No obstructing or sheltering hedges in this very new part of the town, Mr Lawrence observed.

"Oh look!" Lucy said. "Here's the ambulance."

186

It was indeed coming towards them at a good pace, its bell ringing and blue light flashing. At the same moment the front door behind them opened and the three policemen appeared with Mrs Lawrence, ashen-faced, the felt hat pushed to the back of her head, moving woodenly in their midst. In the nearest police car the engine woke with a brisk roar.

What happened next took them all by surprise. All, that is to say, except James Lawrence, who had been brought up on a farm among the mindless, impulsive, violent actions of cattle. He had watched intently and when Dorothy broke away and charged at Lucy in a savage fury he waited until she was upon them, then snatched the girl from her path, so that instead of pushing Lucy into the track of the ambulance, now sweeping in to the kerb, her headlong rush carried her forward and she pitched into the high radiator and was thrown down, the nearside front wheel cracking her spine as it passed over her. She screamed as she fell but more in anger than in pain.

They scooped her very carefully from the road, sliding a blanket under her and drawing it slowly sideways and back until she was clear of the wheels and a stretcher could be moved beneath the blanket. Her face was bloody from a cut on her forehead, but the ambulance had been slowing to a halt when it struck her, the cut was not deep and she was quite conscious. The ambulance men touched her legs. No feeling in them, no movement. Her back was broken and she knew it.

From the stretcher she pointed a hand at Mr Lawrence.

"He pushed me," she whispered to Dow, who bent over her. "Murderer! Pushed me!"

But Dow had seen exactly what had happened. He was both furious and ashamed. He had let her persuade him not to use the bracelets, nor throw a blanket over her

187

head. Three of them with her, he with a hand on her arm. And she had gone in a flash.

"You tried to kill the girl, didn't you?" he said. "Didn't you?"

"Can't prove it. Never prove it. Never have — never — convicted — never — "

She was silent. Shock had taken over. Shock and guilt and total defeat at last. She sank into darkness.

19

DOROTHY LAWRENCE SURVIVED for two years before she died of a virus pneumonia caught in an epidemic at the hospital for incurables where she had been confined since the accident.

For she had never left a hospital ward. She had never been charged with the murder of Jim Binscott, nor with any of her other crimes.

"You can't take them to court in a wheelchair without putting half the jury on their side right away." Sergeant Thomas explained to young Hill. "Not her kind. Look how she diddled the super when she broke loose and dished herself."

"That James Lawrence was quick off the mark. Wot say he did the pushing that time? Wouldn't blame him, would you?"

"I'd give her a medal for doing Binscott. Saved us a lot of trouble, they're all saying. They'd like it to settle nice and quiet. Look out, that cat only just made it! Don't want another bust spine, do you?"

Mrs Chandler's leg was in plaster for several weeks with a first degree Pott's fracture. She was away from the office for three months, suspended on full pay. For a time the two causes of absence mingled, as intended, but details crept out, unpleasant facts were assembled and their nasty smell rose among the higher ranks of the Social Services complex. She had tangled very unfortunately with the police; she had withheld, even to the point of obstruction and untruth, certain knowledge about a client suspected of criminal action. By which they meant obtaining money and services on false pretences, nothing more deadly.

Archie Hill, too, received a warning about his partial obstruction of the police over not declaring Dorothy Lawrence's presence in his area to them. But Mrs Lone saved him from certain dismissal and in the end, in gratitude for her protection, he married her.

By the time Mrs Chandler was walking again, though using a stick, the report condemning her had been accepted, points in her favour had been put, and against the recommendation of the report she had been reinstated in her old job. Her first action, when there, was to fire Beryl and also Margery. She then got Miss Carr transferred to another Group and finding she had lost too much merit in Meadowfield to continue her success there, applied for, and secured, a post in the same area as Elaine Brigg.

James Lawrence went back to Canada as soon as he was free to do so. Until that happened he stayed in Cambridge, driving to Meadowfield when he was needed there but giving his address to no one. He did meet Geoff and Lucy several times, urging them to visit him and his family in Canada or even to emigrate.

"Not yet," Geoff told him and Lucy agreed. They were saddened but not sickened, by the crimes of Mrs Lawrence, they said. She was a real psychopath.

"She killed my father and she got off scot free," Mr Lawrence protested.

"She's got a life sentence," Lucy said, "which is what she'd have had in the courts. Only harder for her. The other patients in her ward won't speak to her."

"She deserved to be hanged," Mr Lawrence insisted.

In later years, when Mr Tine, new editor of the *Meadowfield Advertiser*, wrote an article upon the rise of crime in the neighbourhood, he described the case of Mrs Lawrence, the local psychopath, with her crimes proved or suspected. The town agreed with him.

But Mrs Chandler, on one of her visits to her old friend, Miss Brigg at Seacombe, sometimes walked with her on the pier there, remembering Dorothy as she did so.

"I still believe it was an accident," she said. "They were all accidents. Or could have been."

"Not all, surely?"

"Well, not Binscott, I suppose. But she was driven to it that time. She had great problems. She was not a strong character."

"No, Violet. On the contrary. Frighteningly strong. Evil, I came to the conclusion."

"No one is basically wicked, Elaine. We were taught that and I still believe it. If you had known her you would agree with me. Except at the end, when she was not herself, I always found her such a nice client."

*If you have enjoyed this book, you might
wish to join the Walker British Mystery Society.*

*For information, please send a postcard or
letter to:*

Paperback Mystery Editor

**Walker & Company
720 Fifth Avenue
New York, NY 10019**